DOCTOR WHO

THE WELL

THE CHANGING FACE OF DOCTOR WHO
The cover illustration of this book portrays the Fifteenth DOCTOR WHO.

THE WELL

Based on the BBC television adventure
by Sharma Angel-Walfall and Russell T Davies

GARETH L POWELL

BOOKS

BBC BOOKS

UK | USA | Canada | Ireland | Australia
India | New Zealand | South Africa

BBC Books is part of the Penguin Random House group of companies whose
addresses can be found at global.penguinrandomhouse.com

Penguin Random House UK
One Embassy Gardens, 8 Viaduct Gardens, London SW11 7BW

penguin.co.uk

global.penguinrandomhouse.com

Penguin
Random House
UK

First published by BBC Books in 2025

Doctor Who is produced in Wales by Bad Wolf with BBC Studios Productions.
Executive Producers: Jane Tranter, Julie Gardner, Joel Collins,
Phil Collinson and Russell T Davies

Editorial Director: Albert DePetrillo
Project Editor: Steve Cole
Cover Design: Two Associates
Cover illustration: Dan Liles

Typeset by Rocket Editorial Ltd
Printed and bound in Great Britain by Clays Ltd, Elcograf S.p.A.

The authorised representative in the EEA is Penguin Random House Ireland,
Morrison Chambers, 32 Nassau Street, Dublin D02 YH68

A CIP catalogue record for this book is available from the British Library

ISBN 9781785949562

MIX
Paper | Supporting
responsible forestry
FSC® C018179

Penguin Random House is committed to a sustainable future
for our business, our readers and our planet. This book is made
from Forest Stewardship Council® certified paper.

Contents

Contents

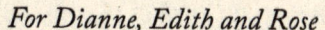

For Dianne, Edith and Rose

Courage isn't just a matter of not being frightened, you know. It's being afraid and doing what you have to do anyway.

The Third Doctor

Prologue
Waiting for the Humans

The presence had been alone for 400,000 years, haunting the caverns and rock fissures deep beneath the blasted surface of its ruined world.

Once upon a time, millennia ago, other creatures came from beyond the sky, in ships made of metal and plastic and fire. They called themselves humans. And while they were able to wield great technological power, they were also fleshy and vulnerable and unable to survive on the surface without their machines.

At first, the presence stalked the periphery of their settlement. It watched the comings and goings of their little vehicles with caterpillar tracks and covered windows. When it felt ready, it found a way inside.

The humans were unprepared, of course.

Before they even suspected what might be happening, the presence clawed its way into their soft and pliable minds and began to feast upon their fear, devour their anger and bask in the nourishing purity of their hatred. In their bright, vibrant memories, it caught tantalising glimpses of other worlds beyond this desolate wasteland. A million worlds, each filled with billions of other such creatures. A trillion opportunities to grow and learn and play.

And feed.

In that moment, it hatched a plan to escape this radioactive hellhole of a planet and spread itself across the stars in an endless frenzy of conquest and predation...

It would have been glorious, but it had been stopped. Prevented by the very creatures it had sought to subjugate. Cast back into exile and solitude.

Now, it paced restlessly in its subterranean confinement, as it had done for the past 400,000 years, slithering through seams in the rock, crawling through cracks and fissures, as it seethed with rage and resentment, waiting for another chance to escape and wreak a terrible vengeance on those who had so unfairly imprisoned it.

Waiting for the arrival of more weak, unwitting humans.

Waiting for another chance to feast.

But most of all, waiting for the creature that called itself... the Doctor.

Chapter 1
Swatted by a Giant Moth

Why did time travel have to be so complicated? There were so many brightly coloured knobs, switches, levers and dials on the main TARDIS console that, sometimes, the Doctor wished he had more than one pair of hands.

That's what friends are for, he thought.

As the blue box careened through the fiery time vortex, he helped Belinda wrap her fingers around two of the most important switches and then moved around to the opposite side of the control console.

Because of course the controls he needed to operate were on opposite sides.

It was going to work this time, he told himself, gripping the lever.

It *had* to work …

He began to count down. 'Five.'

On the other side of the console, resplendent in a wide-skirted yellow swing dress, Belinda bit her lower lip in concentration.

'Four.'

He saw the muscles in her forearms tense, ready to pull her switches.

'Three.'

Distracted for a millisecond or two, the Doctor tried to recall if he'd ever met any Time Lords who had grown an extra pair of arms. Maybe a few extra pairs. He was sure at least one of them must have tried it … These old Type 40 models had originally been designed to be flown by six Time Lords, all working together. Surely the Time Lords could have found a way to replace the entire console with a glass touchscreen that one person could operate without having to stretch themselves around like they were playing Twister. In fact, they could probably have just made the whole TARDIS entirely automatic if they'd wanted to.

But where would be the fun in that?

Time travel, at least the way the Doctor did it, was more an art than a science. More intuition than skill. More luck than judgement.

'Two.'

Here we go …

'One.'

As instructed, Belinda threw her switches. At the same exact instant, the Doctor yanked down the thick silver handle that initiated the landing sequence.

Please work, he pleaded silently. *Please work.*

The glowing lights in the console's central column moved up and down. The engines wheezed and groaned.

Come on, you magnificent machine. Come onnnn …

They were almost there, almost there, but then –

The TARDIS shuddered and … bounced.

The same bounce as last time.

'No!' the Doctor cried in dismay. 'No, no, no, no.' He didn't know why his precious, ancient ship kept flinching away every time he tried to take Belinda home to London in 2025. And if there was one thing the Doctor hated, it was not knowing something.

It was almost as if the universe had placed an impossible, invisible barrier around the entire planet on that date, causing the old ship to glance off every time he tried.

Could the fault be internal?

Despite the shiny new appearance of the control room, the TARDIS had been an antique when he'd stolen her from Gallifrey. Since then, he and the old machine had been through a lot together, travelling back and forth from one end of the space-time continuum to the other, from the Revenant Stars to the Glisten Cascade, and beyond – and maybe, just maybe, it was starting to show its age.

In the last three hours he had stripped down and reassembled the time circuits half a dozen times, and still the TARDIS stubbornly refused to materialise on Earth on May 24th 2025. And he couldn't work out why. Having failed again, they were now spinning randomly through the time vortex. It was maddening.

To his knowledge, nothing momentous was supposed to happen in 2025. No huge disasters or alien invasions – certainly nothing that could cause the entire Earth to get time-locked. So, if it wasn't a time-lock, what was it? Surely nothing good.

From the other side of the console, Belinda saw his consternation and it worried her. 'So, if we can't get home,' she said nervously, 'and if the TARDIS isn't broken, it means … What? Planet Earth is broken, or 2025 is broken?'

The Doctor didn't respond. He was beginning to fear the same thing – because there were only a finite number of reasons the TARDIS might refuse to materialise somewhere, and the utter destruction of that somewhere ranked fairly highly on the list. It had an instinct for self-preservation that caused it to avoid materialising inside exploding stars, hazardous paradoxes and erupting volcanoes.

What if there wasn't a barrier around the Earth, it was just that the world had somehow become so dangerous in 2025 that the TARDIS was refusing to return?

'Have we been invaded?' Belinda went on, sounding increasingly worried. 'Or hit by a meteor? Or swatted by a giant moth?'

That last one caught his attention. Snapped from his reverie, the Doctor's irritation vanished like the sun coming out from behind a cloud, and his eyes shone with delight.

'Imagine a moth that big!' He'd seen some moths in his time, no doubt about that. Tiny little brown ones that ate his socks. Huge, colourful ones with impressive wing spans and furry legs. And then there had been that gigantic one in Tokyo – that had been a monster, bigger than skyscrapers, with wings wider than city blocks.

But he'd never encountered one large enough to swat an entire planet. That would certainly be a sight worth seeing.

Imagine how many socks it could eat!

'But really?' Belinda begged, almost on the verge of tears now. 'Cos my parents are back home, and if this is Friday, then they go to this bar with their mates, and Dad sings, and everyone laughs and then the whole place ends up singing. Every Friday night. Is that still happening, Doctor? Are they safe?'

'I hope so,' the Doctor muttered, meaning it, but still preoccupied by his malfunctioning TARDIS and thoughts of moths the size of nebulae, with wings spun from shimmering starlight.

'You hope …?' Tears filled Belinda's eyes and her hands shook.

The Doctor jerked from his reverie. He hadn't realised how upset she was. Sometimes, it took him a moment to notice things like that.

'Hey.' He pulled her into a tight hug. 'Hey, hey, c'mere.'

Belinda closed her eyes as the Doctor squeezed her comfortingly, then stepped back and took her hands. When she looked at him, she could see the concern and kindness in his eyes. There was no reservation there, no pretence. He wasn't humouring her. His compassion was genuine, and she knew beyond any shred of doubt that he really, honestly did want her to be safe and happy.

'I will meet your mum and dad, one day,' he reassured her. 'I will make your dad laugh, and your mum can whistle at my behind.' He gave a cheeky grin. 'Then I will sing!' His smile widened. 'I'll do the singing! That's a promise.'

'But, you can't promise,' Belinda sniffed. Her parents were both musicians. Her father's pub band played covers to rooms full of middle-aged rhythm and blues enthusiasts, and her mother was a classically trained violinist – or 'fiddle player' as her father insisted on putting it. She found the idea that they might be in some sort of danger intolerable.

'Look at me.' The Doctor leaned in close, fixing her with a serious stare. 'I can,' he said, quietly but insistently, as if reciting incontrovertible facts. 'I will. I do.'

Belinda felt a shiver pass down her spine. The Doctor appeared young, but occasionally, when he spoke like that, the air seemed to crackle with static electricity. No one so young could possibly summon such sincerity, such gravitas. In those moments, she imagined she caught a glimpse of something ancient and determined behind his youthful mask. A well of experience and heartbreak deeper than worlds and time. As if, despite looking like he was in his late twenties or possibly early thirties, he had somehow lived for thousands of years and endured torments beyond imagining and heartaches she couldn't even begin to comprehend.

Perhaps that was why he cared so much. And she could tell he did. He really, truly cared, this wild, energetic, emotional man. He shone with love the way a star shone with light and heat, warming and illuminating everyone around him.

Until a couple of days ago, she'd been a nurse in London, working for the NHS and putting in long hours at the hospital, coping with stretched budgets, annoying housemates and a non-existent love life. Then she'd been kidnapped from home by weird robots and taken to another planet. She knew she'd still be there now, if it hadn't been for the Doctor. He'd burst out of nowhere, saved the day and whirled her away in his time machine.

There was so much about him she didn't know, and she didn't know how much of what he *had* told her was true. And yet, she realised, she was starting to trust him, and starting to believe he could – and would – bend the laws of time and space to keep such a wild promise. And that maybe, if he could do that, he could do *anything*.

He was miraculous. She only had to look at his TARDIS for proof. From the outside, it resembled an old-fashioned blue police telephone box. The sort you might see in an old black and white British movie. Maybe big enough for two people to stand in. But once you got past the doors and stepped inside … Inside, it was *enormous*.

The control room was a shining white dome probably forty metres across, with evenly spaced lights set into the walls and ramps that curved and swooped, linking the main console to the front doors, and to portals that led off into other rooms beyond. The air smelled fresh and clean, like standing beneath a cherry blossom tree after a thunderstorm, and the lights around the dome changed in magnificent ripples of colour that swept up from the floor and down from the ceiling.

Other rooms lay beyond the control room, but they were more of a mystery.

When they'd landed in Miami, the Doctor had shown her the wardrobe, which was a chamber roughly the size of a shopping mall, its levels linked by spiral staircases and its floorspace crammed with rack upon rack of clothing, and its aisles blocked by chaotic heaps of hats and shoes from a thousand different times and cultures. That was where she'd found the chic 1950s get-up she was currently wearing. But beyond the wardrobe, there were still so many more rooms she hadn't yet had the opportunity to explore, and she didn't even know how far back those rooms and corridors extended, or how big the interior of the TARDIS really was. The Doctor occasionally mentioned a library and a pool but was always vague when she asked where they were, telling her he hadn't had time to get used to the 'new layout' yet, whatever that meant. He'd also once referred to something called 'Adric's room' but, when she'd asked who Adric was, he'd immediately changed the subject.

Like the TARDIS, the Doctor had his secrets.

When she was a kid, her dad had told her that people often ended up looking like their cars. Sometimes he said weird things like that when he came home from band practice. On this occasion, though, he might've had a point. Maybe something similar was happening here. Perhaps over the years, the Doctor and his TARDIS had grown to become reflections of one another. Certainly, they were both more than they appeared from the outside. They each had hidden, inaccessible depths, and each seemed to contain so very many memories – some good, some bad. And yet on the surface, they both appeared somehow brand new.

As he held her hands, she looked into his wide, concerned eyes and smiled. His plan was going to work, she told herself. If anyone could get her home, it would be him.

Even as she thought that, the TARDIS groaned and juddered. The lights pulsed on the walls. The column at the centre of the control console slowed its rise and fall, grinding to a halt. There was a final jolt, and then everything went still and silent.

They had arrived somewhere.

Chapter 2
Do We Still Exist?

The Doctor cocked his head, as if listening to something she couldn't hear. He released her hand and sprang into motion, racing over to grab the Vindicator.

'Right, Belinda Chandra,' he said with cheerful resolve. 'We go out there, and we take another Vindicator reading, cos every single reading pulls us closer to home.'

As the TARDIS couldn't seem to get a lock on their destination, the Doctor had built the Vindicator to help. The device was basically a telescoping aerial attached to an elaborately carved tripod. He knew that Belinda thought it resembled a steampunk version of one of those cheesy Flying V electric guitars that rock bands used to play in the 1980s. It even had a strap to make it easy for the Doctor to sling it over his shoulder. But while it looked absurdly simple, like all Time Lord technology the mechanisms inside were fiendishly complex.

Wherever the TARDIS landed, he used the device to take a four-dimensional fix on the Earth in 2025. He'd already taken one reading in Miami in the 1950s, and now he was going to take another from here, wherever 'here' might be. He hoped that, by triangulating these readings (if triangulate was the right word when talking about four-dimensional coordinates), the TARDIS would be able to pinpoint their target precisely and hopefully materialise without bouncing off.

'But where have we landed?' Belinda asked, thinking it might be an idea to at least know that before they stepped outside.

The Doctor bent over the console and studied the instruments.

'Whoa!' His eyebrows leapt up. 'Five hundred thousand years in the future.' His face broke into a delighted smile. 'We have *jumped*, baby!'

Belinda opened and shut her mouth in surprise. She could scarcely believe it. 'But that's massive. That's …' She tried to imagine being so far ahead of her own time, to picture all the things that could have happened over such a long intervening period.

For goodness' sake, it had taken modern humans less time than that to go from existing as a few isolated tribes of hunter-gatherers to a species capable of landing on the moon.

Think what they might have become by now! Think of the advances they might have made in medicine and healthcare.

Perhaps disease was a thing of the past, and they were all living hundreds of years. Perhaps they all had jetpacks and flying cars and printers that didn't chew up the paper when you were trying to print out an important document.

Half a million years was time enough for anything to have happened.

Anything...

Wait.

A chill crept down her spine as she thought about all the mistakes of the past.

'Do we still exist?' She stumbled over her words, worried humanity might have fallen prey to climate change, or another pandemic, or wiped itself out in a stupid war. 'I mean me, I mean human beings. Is there still a human race in 500,000 years?'

'There's always a human race,' the Doctor said, eyes shining with something like paternal pride. 'You voyage out there and own it. Far and wide, right across the stars.'

، He closed his eyes in a moment of contented contemplation. Then he held out an inviting hand to her, and his smile flashed like summer lightning. 'Come and see.'

Belinda felt a thrill of excitement. She was so excited to see where they were but … they were 500,000 years in the future!

'Wait,' she said, hesitating. 'Do they speak English out there? Is English still a thing?'

The Doctor tapped his ear. 'The TARDIS translates. Try it!'

Okay, that took care of one problem.

But Belinda looked down at her outfit. It had been great in 1950s America, but she didn't think people would still be wearing cinch-waisted yellow swing dresses half a million years in the future. If they were all wearing sparkly silver jumpsuits or ripped road warrior leather, she was going to look like an idiot.

'Do we get to change our clothes?' she asked.

The Doctor glanced at his old-fashioned blue blazer and pink bow tie as if just remembering he was still wearing it. He looked up slyly and raised an eyebrow. 'Girl, you're beginning to enjoy this!' His teeth flashed in an exultant grin. 'At last!' He put down the Vindicator and took her hand. 'C'mon!'

Laughing, they hurried down one of the curving ramps, to the lowest portal in the room.

* * *

The two of them emerged from the portal at the top of the highest ramp.

Belinda looked down in amazement at the futuristic gear the TARDIS seemed to have picked out for them. They were both now wearing tight, smart, deep-blue one-piece spacesuits with body armour on the shoulders, chests and knees, and they each had a pair of big, chunky space boots.

'Come on!' the Doctor yelled in appreciation.

'Okay,' she had to agree. 'This is a good look.'

Overjoyed, they ran down the ramp together. The Doctor slung the Vindicator over his shoulder like a rock star would his guitar, then they crossed to the TARDIS doors and stepped out.

The Doctor looked around. He and Belinda were in a long, narrow, grid-metal corridor. Alarms sounding. Distant voices shouting. Running footsteps.

Behind them, the TARDIS nestled in an alcove. Before them was nothing but the other wall, which held a rack of space helmets. If they'd been moving any faster, they would have run straight into it. There wasn't much room: the passage was only wide enough for one person. If two people tried to walk in opposite directions, one of them would have to duck into the alcove now occupied by the TARDIS in order to let the other pass.

The Doctor looked left and right.

From the vibration in the floor, he deduced they were on a spaceship of some kind. The alarms and lights and distant shouts all suggested that maybe they hadn't arrived at the best time.

Or, he thought, *perhaps it's the perfect time.*

In fact, he could scarcely remember the last occasion when he'd set foot on a spaceship that hadn't been in some kind of desperate trouble. People often said flying was the safest way to travel but, in his experience, these things were always crashing or exploding or being overtaken by Weeping Angels – and then crashing and exploding.

More alarms sounded, and he thought, *I know this song …*

The first thing he had to do was find the control room or bridge. From there, he could figure out what was happening and what they were dealing with. Perhaps he'd even find a captain he could speak to. And if this ship was in trouble, he would try to save it.

But would the bridge be to the left or to the right? This ship wasn't a make or model he recognised, though it had a smell of humans about it.

Of course, a surprising number of species in the galaxy shared the general average height and heads-arms-legs shape that characterised human beings. Over the eons, many Time Lord philosophers had speculated on possible reasons for this preponderance of humanoid life, and there had been two main schools of thought. The first proposed the idea that, somehow, the humanoid body plan conferred an evolutionary advantage of some kind, making it particularly suited to the physical laws of the universe, which explained why it kept cropping up again and again. Left to its own devices, evolution would always end up with something basically human-shaped. The other, not necessarily contrary, explanation was that Time Lords had been travelling back and forth throughout the cosmos for so long that they had somehow left a mark on the fabric of reality – a pattern or niche that other life forms had unknowingly adopted.

Personally, the Doctor wasn't convinced by either of these theories. He thought they were both a bit pompous and self-serving. After all, there were life forms out there that looked nothing like humans or Time Lords and still managed to live successful, happy lives. Dolphins, for instance. They knew how to have a great time in the ocean without having to bother with arms and legs and blue jeans and taxes. And those gasbag creatures that floated in the Rose-Coloured Clouds of Maphalanx. They were shaped like airships the length of football pitches, but they were also some of the wisest and most serene beings he'd ever encountered, and amazingly interesting conversationalists – not to mention, inveterate gossips.

Over his many incarnations, he himself had been tall and short, old and young, black and white, male and female … People came in all shapes and sizes and, as far as he was concerned, it didn't matter what anybody looked like, as long as they were having a good time.

So, left or right?

There were hatches at each end of the corridor, and those hatches had to lead somewhere, so he might as well pick the closest. He didn't want to have to squeeze past Belinda in the narrow space.

Before he could take a step, five armed soldiers in identical body armour came filing in from the end of the corridor nearest to him. At the same time, five more marched in from the end closest to Belinda. They appeared human, and their uniforms matched the ones he and Belinda wore.

He gave them a friendly smile. 'Hiya. Hope you don't mind.' He put his hand to his chest. 'I'm the Doctor, and this is my friend, Belinda.'

The soldiers ignored him. They marched in until they were standing in front of the Doctor and Belinda, at which point they clattered to a stop and turned sharply to face the wall. Their boots clanged on the metal floor as they stamped to attention.

Unsure what else to do, the Doctor and Belinda politely copied, standing shoulder-to-shoulder with five soldiers on each side of them.

Belinda tried to explain to them all. 'We're just popping in, really.'

There was no response. The soldiers remained at attention, eyes fixed straight ahead, staring at a row of space helmets lining a long shelf on the wall.

An eleventh trooper entered through one of the hatches. A little older than the rest, this one was definitely in charge; the Doctor could tell by the badges of rank on her sleeve and the way she carried herself with an unmistakable authority.

'Helmets!' she barked.

The troopers reached out and each took a helmet. With practised ease, they slid them over their heads. There was a loud hiss and a short sucking sound as the bottom of each helmet bonded with the collar of its trooper's suit, forming an instant, airtight seal.

The Doctor didn't like what that implied. The only reason to need an airtight suit was if you were expecting to be going somewhere where you'd need to have your own air supply. He picked up the helmet in front of him. It was a standard fishbowl affair, with two powerful lights and a clear crystal visor.

'Better had,' he told Belinda.

They put the helmets over their heads the same way the soldiers had done and heard the same hiss and *schunk!* as the helmets sealed to the necks of their armoured suits.

* * *

The inside of Belinda's helmet smelled like a new car: plastic and metal and rubber, and a lingering hint of garlic and onions. She wrinkled her nose. The last soldier to wear this should have cleaned their teeth after eating.

She was about to open her mouth to ask what would happen next when the officer yelled, 'And jump, jump, jump!'

'What?' The Doctor's head snapped around in alarm. 'What? What?'

'What d'you mean, jump?' Belinda cried.

Before anybody could reply, the wall in front of them slid upwards. They hadn't been standing in a corridor at all. This was an airlock!

Side-by-side with the soldiers, the Doctor and Belinda stood on the brink of a howling void of darkness, wind and swirling gases, with no sign of ground below.

The soldier beside Belinda put his hand on her back.

'No!' she protested. 'But we're not—'

She felt a shove, and the entire squad leapt forwards into the darkness.

As he tumbled with the others, the Doctor caught glimpses of the spaceship they'd jumped from, and his hearts sank as he recognised it as a troop carrier. A tough, utilitarian military design, built to transport soldiers to wherever they were needed and drop them into the heart of the action.

Which meant he and Belinda could be falling towards a battlefield – or worse.

And he didn't even know how to activate the parachute.

Beside him, Belinda started to scream.

He couldn't help joining in.

Chapter 3
Colony Base 15

Down and down they fell, spinning and tumbling.

Even while screaming, part of the Doctor's mind analysed the problem. They were falling towards something, which most likely meant they were dropping towards a planetary surface. Based on the rate of their descent, he made a guess at the strength of the planet's mavity. Then he ran that information through a complicated calculation involving the number of seconds they had been in freefall and came up with an estimate that they had so far fallen 30,000 feet.

30,100.

30,200.

Surely, thought the Doctor, they would reach the ground soon. These were military suits, designed to keep their inhabitants alive and ready for combat. In which case, he reasoned, the other vital systems should be equally foolproof – meaning that whatever must slow their fall should kick in on automatic, like the neck seal.

30,500.

Far below, he caught sight of a rocky, desolate landscape roaring up towards them.

Okay, he thought. *Let's hope I'm right.*

As if in answer, he heard a loud hiss. Little blasts of gas puffed from the elbows, hips and knees of his suit, swinging him around until his feet faced the ground.

31,000.

The Doctor felt a surge of relief. They were going to survive.

Smiling, he reached out and took Belinda's hand. The gas venting from their suits gradually slowed them until they were drifting downwards quite gently.

Just like Mary Poppins!

As their boots crunched onto the planet's surface, the gas jets cut out and Belinda stumbled.

'Whoa, there.' Getting used to a new mavity strength was never easy. The Doctor caught her before she could fall and supported her weight as she sank to her knees. Inside her helmet, her eyes were wide, and she looked totally freaked out. He was worried she might be sick, and that was something you *really* didn't want to do in a sealed space helmet.

26

'Oh my god,' she gasped over the suit-to-suit radio. 'Life. With. You.'

The Doctor had already recovered both his composure and his curiosity. He planted the Vindicator on the ground and pressed the button to activate it.

'I know, I know,' he replied, patting her gloved hand and only half listening. 'But look ...'

Belinda raised her head, and her shock at falling out of a spaceship evaporated as she took in their surroundings.

Her mouth fell open.

They had landed in a harsh and dramatic landscape of plunging canyons, vertical cliffs and rocky towers. Boulders the size of houses lay scattered like dice long since thrown and forgotten, their sides smoothed and sculpted into weird, ethereal shapes by wind and sand. Sharp mountain peaks stood on the horizon like the teeth of a saw. It was a wild, hard wasteland quite unlike anywhere on Earth. Terrifyingly bleak, yet beautiful in its desolation. A ringed planet hung in the sky like a magnificent Christmas bauble, and bright stars shone through the gaps in ragged nebulae the colour of sunset.

Captivated by the stark, eerie landscape, she climbed unsteadily to her feet beside the Doctor. Behind his faceplate, she could see his eyes sparkling as he stood and gazed, equally entranced by the jagged mountains and plunging ravines.

This was what he lived for, Belinda realised. For moments like this, when he laid his eyes on a new horizon for the first time, and stood where no one else had ever stood.

Looking out over the breathtaking peaks and gullies before her, she had to admit she could relate to that. Right now, she could have been working a long shift at the hospital, treating patients and fighting an avalanche of paperwork. Instead, here she was, Belinda Chandra from London, England: 31 years old and dressed as a space marine on the surface of an alien world!

But while she wore the armour of a futuristic soldier, those around her were the real deal. How were they going to react when they discovered two intruders in their midst?

Zzzzz-uppp! The unmistakable sound of weapons powering up. It came from behind, echoing over the suit-to-suit radio.

The Doctor and Belinda turned and found themselves facing eleven laser guns, all pointing directly at them.

'Explain yourselves,' demanded the woman who had given the order to jump. 'Immediately!'

* * *

The Doctor didn't hesitate. His body armour had a number of recessed equipment panels designed for carrying survival gear and extra ammunition. Earlier, he'd stashed his wallet in one of them. Now that panel hissed open and he pulled the wallet out.

With the practised ease of a police detective on a TV show, he flipped it open to reveal a blank piece of psychic paper behind a plastic cover. He held it up so the troopers could see it.

'I'm the Doctor,' he said. 'And this is Nurse Belinda Chandra. Who is your commanding officer back at base?'

'General Chinchappa,' the woman replied.

The Doctor held the paper closer to her. 'I am higher than Chinchappa, see?'

She glared at the paper, and Belinda thought maybe the Doctor's bluff had failed. But then, to her surprise and considerable relief, the woman lowered her weapon.

'Apologies,' she said. 'I'm Platoon Leader Shaya Costallion. I was not informed of your presence.'

The Doctor smiled and tucked the wallet back into the panel on his chest.

Belinda could scarcely believe it. Somehow, this Shaya Costallion had seen something in the Doctor's blank sheet of paper that had convinced her he was an officer.

Feeling a sudden surge of confidence, she decided to join in. 'That's the point,' she said. 'We're like mystery shoppers. Now, we just need to vindicate—'

The Vindicator let out a loud ping. 'Done,' he said. 'We're vindicated.'

'And then you can return us to our blue box,' Belinda continued. 'Which is … on your ship-thing. In the sky.' She sensed she was losing credibility, so tried to copy the tone Shaya had used. 'Immediately!'

The Platoon Leader's brows furrowed in puzzlement. 'How are we supposed to do that?'

The Doctor and Belinda gave each other a desperate look, both hoping the other had an answer. They'd managed to wing it this far, but now they were stuck.

'Oh,' Shaya said, as if just realising something. 'Oh, this is a test.'

'Yes!' the Doctor cried in relief.

'Yes,' Belinda agreed. 'Yes, that's right!'

Shaya motioned to her troopers, and they all lowered their weapons.

'This is Planet 6-7-6-7,' she said formally, obviously reciting the mission briefing. 'And the atmosphere, what little of it there is, is charged with galvanic radiation. It would strip the engines bare. The ship needs to slide down at retrograde velocity.'

The Doctor smiled at her encouragingly. 'Which will take …?'

'Five hours.'

'Okay,' Belinda said. 'We've got five hours.' That didn't seem so bad. They could have a look around, she supposed, and see the sights. After all, it wasn't every day she found herself on a new planet – even one as barren and wild as this. Then a worrying thought struck her, and she asked, 'Can we breathe for five hours?'

Shaya looked surprised by the question. 'You can breathe in that suit for five months.'

'Correct answer,' Belinda said in some relief. 'Good.'

Beside her, the Doctor frowned. 'So …' he said. 'Just imagine I know nothing about this mission. Tell me from scratch. What the hell are you doing here? Cos galvanic radiation is tough. Nothing could live on a rock like this, but you've come all this way.' He fixed Shaya with an inquisitive stare. 'What for?'

Shaya held his gaze for a few seconds. Then she turned and led him and Belinda over to the edge of the nearest ravine.

'Colony Base 15,' she said, pointing.

Colony Base 15 stood at the bottom of a wide fissure, about a mile away. Most of the outpost seemed to be contained under a central dome, although the Doctor could see a few attached outbuildings, some huge excavators with caterpillar tracks, a row of half-constructed derricks and a large tower reaching into the sky beside the dome.

To his eye, it looked like the top of a mineshaft, and a red light blinked at its summit.

'Basic mining operation,' Shaya continued, confirming his guess. 'With a mercury drop-line, stripping out a layer of carbon-46.' She shrugged. 'But then, 15 days ago, all contact was lost.'

A few lights were on in the dome, but the Doctor couldn't see any movement. Nobody walking around. No machinery in use. Everything looked quiet and still. Deserted.

'How many colonists?' he asked.

'Thirty-five.' Shaya turned to one of her team. 'Trooper 3, any signs of life?'

Trooper 3 looked young. Perhaps in her mid-twenties. Glyphs on her suit identified her as Mo Gilliben.

'Nothing,' Mo replied. 'No movement. No damage to the dome. We can't scan for heartbeats because of the radiation, so there's still hope.'

'Hope is irrelevant, thank you,' Shaya snapped. 'Troopers, advance.'

The soldiers folded away their scanners, raised their weapons and moved off, down the hill towards the base.

The Doctor and Belinda exchanged a worried glance and followed.

PERSONNEL FILE

NAME	Shaya Costallion
RANK	Platoon Leader
AGE	34
PLACE OF BIRTH	Lombardo Wildlands

PROFILE
Orphaned during the Retáliation at Miller's Ridge, Costallion joined the Colonial Defence Militia in her teens and saw combat during the disastrous Rout of the Seven Dragons.

An exemplary marksman, Costallion served as a sniper during the Outer Reach campaign and is credited with having neutralised over 100 enemy combatants before being seriously wounded during the Drakenfield Skirmish.

Returning to duty in time for the Battle of Hero's Spike, she gained a field promotion to the rank of Platoon Leader in Forward Reconnaissance under General Chinchappa.

ASSESSMENT
A highly professional and ruthless leader, and extremely loyal to the troopers under her command, Costallion is driven by a strong desire to excel at all costs. However, General Chinchappa has expressed concern that this need for perfection occasionally interferes with her ability to make rapid on-the-spot judgement calls.

Chapter 4
Broken Glass

With a growing sense of foreboding, the Doctor trailed along behind the soldiers, and Belinda followed him. Covering the distance to the dome took a little over half an hour. The going was slow because the rocky surface was jagged and uneven. At one point, they had to detour around a chasm so deep the bottom of it was lost in darkness. Then they had to pass through a labyrinth of tall rocky outcrops. Thousands of years of sandblasting had worn channels between these outcrops, leaving them thin at the bottom and wider at the top, like disturbingly organic-looking stone fungi, and the thin, barely extant wind keened between them, throwing grit and dust through the arcs of light from their helmet lamps.

By the time they reached the base, Belinda's legs were tired from trudging and her feet uncomfortably hot and sore inside her boots.

The light from a small orange safety beacon guided them past generators and parked utility vehicles to the dome's external airlock.

'Maximum six personnel,' Gilliben reported, pointing to a sign over the outer door.

'Okay,' Shaya said, 'Troopers 1, 2 and 3, you're with me. The rest of you, stay alert and follow us through.' She turned to the Doctor and Belinda. 'And if you'd care to step this way?'

They filed inside the metal-walled chamber, and Mo Gilliben pressed the button that closed the external hatch.

Apparently, Belinda had seen enough sci-fi on TV to know how an airlock worked, and the Doctor watched her listen to the series of hisses and groans the machinery made behind the walls as the radioactive atmosphere from outside was sucked out of the lock and breathable air pumped in.

When the pressure in the chamber matched that inside the base, the light above the inner door turned green and the lock disengaged with a solid clunk.

Trooper 1, whose suit glyphs identified him as Cassio Palin-Paleen, led the way with his gun raised and Trooper 2, Kai Sabba, right behind.

They found themselves in an antechamber constructed of metal grids and ductwork. A medical kit and a fire extinguisher were bolted to the wall beside the airlock door. A row of tough, industrial-looking pressure suits hung in alcoves on the wall, sagging open like flayed ghosts. The main lights were off and the overhead emergency lights suffused everything with an unsettling orange hue.

There had been no attempt to decorate or make the interior of the base look welcoming. This was unmistakably a working environment, and everything in it had been designed to be durable and functional, as befitted an industrial installation.

'Trooper 2,' Cassio instructed, consulting a virtual map. 'Sortie. Take Walkway One. Any threat to life, you have permission. Shoot to kill.'

Kai threw a salute and stepped through the hatch that led into the rest of the base, keeping his weapon at the ready.

Years ago, the Doctor's friend Sarah Jane Smith had commented that you always knew you were getting old when the policemen started looking young. Well, that went double for soldiers and, compared to the Doctor, Shaya and her troopers were all children. He was almost incalculably older than them, and when he looked at Kai, he felt every one of those years weighing down on him.

How could kids like this put themselves in harm's way right at the start of their lives, before they'd had a chance to really live? They couldn't even regenerate if they were seriously injured.

As the young man's footsteps clanked away into the darkness beyond the hatch, Shaya closed the airlock's inner door.

'Troopers 4 to 9,' she said over the comms channel, 'follow us in. Trooper 10, maintain exterior guard.'

She pressed the button to cycle the airlock, and the light above the inner door turned red as the pumps sucked the breathable air out again, ready for the others to gain access from outside.

'Internal team, unmask,' Cassio ordered.

'Discard flight-packs,' Shaya added.

Cassio, Shaya and Mo removed their helmets, the airtight seals breaking as easily as they had formed, and shrugged out of their flight harnesses.

The Doctor and Belinda copied them. As Belinda pulled her helmet upwards, it gave a sucking hiss and pop, like a cork being pulled from a wine bottle, and came free. She shook out her hair in relief, glad to be out of the confines of the fishbowl and free from the odours of its last user – even if the air in here smelled stale and metallic.

Following the troopers' example, they placed their helmets on a rack beside the lock, and the Doctor shrugged off the Vindicator and slid it onto a shelf where it would be safe.

'I keep thinking,' Belinda said. 'This planet's uninhabited. But they're *mining*. Can something live underground?'

The Doctor shook his head. 'Impossible. The radiation soaks through everything, all the way to the core. We're only safe in here because it's shielded. This whole world is cold and dead and lifeless, and yet ...'

He began to unfasten the top layer of his body armour, dropping shoulder pads and the metal chest piece onto the floor as they came free. Seeing him, Belinda started to copy, and he helped her with the clips she couldn't easily reach.

'You should stay suited,' Cassio warned. He was older than the other two troopers. Maybe in his early thirties, Belinda guessed.

The Doctor dropped the last elbow pad. 'Not loving the look, thanks babe.' Armour shed, he was left with just the blue bodysuit. 'I come in peace.'

Cassio's face hardened. 'It's not appropriate to call me "babe".'

The Doctor flashed him a grin. 'Okay, honey.'

He knew he was pushing his luck, but there was something about the military mind that often brought out the worst in him. These children could run around with their guns, thinking their training and armour made them invincible and their little sacrifices mattered in the grand scheme of things. But, over the course of his many lives, the Doctor had fought in more horrific wars than these youngsters could ever imagine.

He had seen whole star systems incinerated. Entire species erased. Great civilisations destroyed.

And that was why he refused to take this man's ideas of appropriateness seriously.

I am the Doctor, he thought, *and if I want to call you honey, big man, there's nothing you can do about it, okay?*

Cassio's cheeks reddened, but before he could formulate a response, Kai reappeared at the hatchway.

'We have a body,' he said.

The figure lay face-down on the metal gridwork deck of Walkway Two. Instinctively, Belinda went to check the body.

'Don't touch them,' Shaya ordered.

'No, but they might be alive.' It didn't matter what kind of situation Belinda was in, she couldn't stand back if someone needed help. That was just who she was. Who she always had been, right from childhood. She'd always be the first one to assist when one of her classmates felt ill or tripped and grazed their knee in the playground. It was that need to get involved and make a difference that had drawn her into nursing in the first place.

Now she let her training guide her as she crouched beside the body. Their clothes smelled musty, like rags left too long in an attic. As a nurse, she knew the first thing she had to do was check if they were breathing.

She bent down and saw the body's face was that of a man. She placed her cupped hand beneath his nostrils. Nothing.

That might mean his airway was obstructed. She needed to turn him over so she could try to clear it. But she needed to check for spinal injuries before she could move him.

She reached out to touch the skin at the back of his neck. It was cold and loose beneath her fingers, and the bones in his neck crunched and scraped like broken glass in a brown paper bag. She snatched back her hands.

'Oh,' she said, wiping her fingers on her thighs. 'No, sorry. Okay. They've been dead for a while.' She felt a pang of sorrow. By the looks of him, he had lain here for days in this empty walkway, untouched and slowly shrivelling. It seemed such a sad and lonely way to die.

'I'm sorry,' she told him, genuinely regretful. 'We were too late.'

The Doctor crouched to look. 'I'd say they've broken their neck,' he said, frowning as he checked further down. 'Or … broken everything?'

The most cursory of inspections confirmed it; the pelvis had shattered, and every rib was broken, as if the body had hit the floor hard enough to flatten the ribcage until it gave way. But there simply wasn't room in this corridor for it to have fallen that far – which meant either it had suffered a fall elsewhere and then been brought here, or it had been crushed by something either very heavy or very strong.

Right now, he thought. *Right now is the moment we should turn around and go wait outside to be picked up. Just say nope, step back and walk away.*

But he knew the soldiers wouldn't leave, and neither would he. An isolated mining colony and an impossible corpse? How was he supposed to walk away from that? It was way too tantalising.

Shaya directed her squad – and the two strangers – to move on. She aimed to get to the Central Control Room, which was where she expected any survivors to have gathered. Or, if no one had survived, at least she might be able to access the security footage that would confirm what had happened to the crew.

Up until now, it had been possible that some kind of mechanical failure or broken communications equipment could have been responsible for the base's silence. But now that they'd found a body, Shaya could feel the heightened tension among her troopers.

It wasn't so much the discovery of the dead man that bothered her. From the extent of his injuries, she guessed he'd maybe been crushed in some sort of industrial accident. These things happened on isolated mining stations, where health and safety budgets were small, and the rules tended to be laxly enforced. The thing that unsettled her was the way he had been left in a corridor instead of being buried or put into storage. Why had his crewmates dragged him halfway to the airlock and then just dumped him?

As they advanced along Walkway Two, Shaya stole a sideways glance at the Doctor. Was all this – the base, the dead body – still part of a test? She knew Chinchappa had given her command of this mission in order to give her a chance to prove herself, but now it seemed someone higher up the chain of command had taken an interest and sent this Doctor to assess her performance. Had he set up this entire elaborate scenario as some kind of riddle, to see how she responded to a mysterious and possibly lethal mystery?

She knew she was being paranoid, but was she being paranoid enough? Clawing her way up the ranks of non-commissioned officers to the position of platoon leader had taken her ten hard, frustrating years. Only exceptional candidates advanced higher.

Chinchappa thought she took too long to make important command decisions. He called it dithering, but she preferred to think of it as taking a moment to evaluate all the available data. She would rather take an extra half-second to consider all the options before committing her squad to the wrong course of action. In combat, an officer's judgement call could lead to catastrophic losses if they'd missed a vital piece of intelligence. History was littered with military blunders that could have been avoided if those in charge had simply taken a step back to consider the bigger picture.

As platoon leader, the lives of her squad were in her hands, and she took that responsibility very seriously. These were her people, and she would order them to their deaths if she had to – but only if there was no other choice. She had seen too many young lives needlessly thrown onto the bonfire of history by the incompetence of their commanding officers.

I'll be damned if I'm going to make the same mistake, Shaya thought.

Shortly after her fourteenth birthday, the Lombardic War of Unification had come to her village in the Wildlands. First there had been an aerial bombardment, then the ground had shaken with the rumble of oncoming tanks. One or the other of the competing factions – they were very difficult to tell apart – had designated her little cluster of cabins and shacks a strategic military target and had become determined to capture it.

The first tank shell had killed her father outright. One moment, he was trying to beat out the flames licking at the roof of their house; the next, he was gone, along with a sizeable chunk of the wall.

'Run, Shaya,' her mother had urged, gripping her upper arms so tightly. 'Run, girl, and hide.'

And so Shaya had run.

She had been the fastest in her village, maybe the fastest in the whole world. And she had run. Oh, how she had run. Barefoot through smoke and fire and battle; through gutted, smouldering ruins and fields of trampled crops. Past the stinking, flyblown remains of slaughtered livestock and the twisted metal of a downed helicopter. She ran and she ran, and then later, when she was too hungry and exhausted to run any further, she lay down and waited to die.

Three days later, a column of Lombardic soldiers stumbled upon her and allowed her to enlist in return for some hot food and clean clothes.

She had been a soldier ever since. For over half her life, the military had given her purpose and a sense of belonging. And it had taught her that snap decisions sometimes cost lives.

So for now, test or not, she wasn't going to rush to prejudge the situation. She was going to collect information and then choose how to act.

No rash choices.

They already had one dead civilian, and she made a silent vow that she would do everything in her power to ensure no one else perished here.

If this was all some kind of charade to see whether she had what it took to be an officer, then she was determined that she would do her best and ensure her squad did everything by the book.

As they stepped into Walkway Three, Belinda was horrified to see four more bodies lying strewn across the deck.

With the Doctor beside her, she followed Cassio and Kai as they advanced along the corridor. The two men stepped gingerly over the scattered corpses, their weapons held ready to respond to any threat.

The Doctor and Belinda stooped to examine the dead.

'This one's been shot,' the Doctor said. 'Laser fire, in the back.'

A little further along, Belinda noticed charred holes between the shoulder blades of the next victim. 'This one's been shot, too. Poor soul.'

There was a lump in her throat that she couldn't swallow, her knees shook and her stomach felt like a pit. As a nurse, she was no stranger to death. She just wasn't used to seeing the evidence of so much violence, all in one place.

These had all been living, breathing people. People with friends and loved ones and jobs. But then something unspeakably violent had happened, leaving them crumpled and smashed on the cold metal floor of this lonely outpost.

By now, the second batch of troopers had cycled through the airlock and caught up. Shaya ordered them to bring up the rear and guard their six while she and Trooper 3, Mo Gilliben, accompanied the Doctor and Belinda.

Mo looked to be about Belinda's age, with kind eyes and a friendliness that peeped out from behind her professional military demeanour. Belinda liked her immediately.

The Doctor moved to the third body. From what Belinda could see, it was a woman with short white hair. Tools had spilled across the floor from her work belt, forming an untidy halo of wrenches, screwdrivers and cable ties.

'This one's …' The Doctor checked the back of her overalls for burn marks. 'No laser fire.' He ran his sonic screwdriver over her head and shoulders and squinted at the device. 'Another broken neck, I think.'

Keeping tight rein on her emotions, as she had been trained, Belinda crossed to the fourth, a man. He lay awkwardly, one arm bent unnaturally behind his back and one of his lower legs sticking out at an odd angle.

He looked like a rag doll that had been picked up and repeatedly dashed to the ground by an angry child.

'It's like his limbs have been … snapped.' Belinda shuddered. 'Whatever did this was strong.'

'Half of them have been shot,' said Shaya, behind her. 'And half of them have been battered. What sort of fight is that?'

As the Doctor entered the next walkway, he saw it was part of the base's accommodation section and was lined with bedrooms. The troopers took up guard positions at either end of the corridor while he and Shaya investigated the first room.

Inside, it was small and cramped, with bunks recessed into the wall and a fold-down hygiene station. A body lay slumped face-down in a pile of debris beside the bunks. Around it lay a mess of clothes, the smashed remnants of a computer pad, several broken picture frames and the glinting shards of a smashed shaving mirror.

'The place is trashed,' the Doctor said. 'There must have been a fight.' He scratched his chin. 'But why?' These people had been miners, not soldiers. What could have caused them to turn on each other with such ferocity?

They made way for Belinda, who pushed past them and knelt to examine the dead man.

While she was doing that, they moved on to the second bedroom. This one looked neater, but the Doctor noticed that like the first bedroom, there was broken glass scattered on the floor.

'Nothing in here,' Shaya said.

Behind them, in the first room, Belinda called out, 'This one's got a broken neck.'

The Doctor's earlier feeling of foreboding returned tenfold. Given the catastrophic severity of their injuries, it was almost impossible that another person could have caused them, no matter how violent the brawl.

He glanced into the third room. The layout in here was the same as the other two, and it had been wrecked as thoroughly as the first, with clothes and possessions everywhere, as if someone had purposefully rifled through, looking for something.

Another dead woman lay propped in a sitting position with her back against the lower bunk and a laser burn through the chest of her overalls. She had socks on her feet but her boots were still under the bunk. She must have been getting dressed when she was shot.

'This one's laser fire,' the Doctor called sadly.

If the personnel on this base had been fighting something strong enough to break necks and smash bones, why had they been firing at each other?

He bent and read the silver dog tags around the woman's neck.

'Chalona Rosani.' He sighed. 'I'm sorry, Chalona. We'll work this out, sweetheart. I promise.'

From behind him, in the second bedroom, Belinda said, 'Doctor?'

'Yes?'

'All this glass. They broke the mirrors. All of them, in every single room. There are no intact mirrors.'

The Doctor turned to the hygiene station. Above it, where you might logically expect a mirror, he saw only the bare metal wall and a couple of screws that might once have held something in place. Below, shards and splinters of glass glinted in the sink and on the floor, crunching under his boot.

From the next room along, Shaya said. 'You're right, same here.'

The Doctor stepped out into the corridor and the two women joined him.

'All the mirrors broken,' Shaya said.

'And everyone dead,' Belinda added.

'What happened here?' the Doctor wondered.

For the moment, he only knew as much as the others: that they were trapped in a closed facility whose previous inhabitants had apparently all killed each other while fighting both one another *and* a mysterious and deadly force.

To anyone else, the prospect would have been horrifying, but to the Doctor, it felt like an old, familiar dance.

How many times had he been in a similar situation, cut off from the outside world, trapped in a remote, sealed installation with a small group of frightened humans while something otherworldly stalked the shadows and picked them off, one by one?

He knew how to do this tango.

If there were monsters in here with them, he would be ready.

Led by Shaya and Cassio, the team progressed through to the fifth walkway. They were moving faster now that they were getting closer to the control room.

As they moved, the Doctor looked around at the troopers. With their helmets on, they had appeared almost identical. Now they were inside and no longer behind glass faceplates, he could see the differences between them.

As well as those he knew by name – Shaya, Cassio, Kai and Mo – there was Trooper 5, who was very tall; Trooper 6, who looked more like a schoolteacher than a soldier; and Trooper 8, who looked older and probably more experienced than a lot of the others, including Cassio. Which made the Doctor wonder why he hadn't been promoted.

'What if no one's alive?' Belinda asked. 'What do we do then?'

Cassio glanced back at her. He had short, black hair and a hardness about his eyes. 'What we should have done in the first place,' he said contemptuously. 'Nuke this site from orbit.'

They reached a T-shaped junction. One way led to the control room and the other to a heavy metal hatch with a big wheel-shaped locking mechanism, submarine-style.

Mo pointed her scanner at the hatch, and it began to beep. She held up her fist. 'There's a heartbeat.'

Everyone stopped.

'At arms!' Shaya barked. And there was a clatter as the troopers brought their weapons to bear.

'Single heartbeat,' Mo reported. 'Inside that room.'

'Could be a survivor,' Belinda suggested.

'Could be the killer,' Shaya replied.

The Doctor looked from one to the other. 'Could be both,' he said.

Determinedly, he marched forwards, illuminated by the lights attached to the troopers' guns, and before anyone could tell him to stop, he seized the iron wheel and turned. The door *clunked* as the lock disengaged, and then its hinges screeched as it swung open.

Head high and chin thrust forwards, the Doctor stepped through.

PERSONNEL FILE

NAME: Cassio Palin-Paleen
RANK: Deputy Platoon Leader
AGE: 30
PLACE OF BIRTH: Central City, Morag

PROFILE

Palin-Paleen completed his basic training at the top
of his class, with distinctions in Technology and Hand-
to-Hand Combat.

He first saw combat during the Battle of Skull Moon,
and served with distinction during actions at Lizard
Canyon and the Southern Mountain Fastness.

In the aftermath of Hero's Spike, he was assigned to Forward Reconnaissance, under Platoon Leader Shaya Costallion, where he currently serves as her second-in-command.

ASSESSMENT

Palin-Paleen is an extremely ambitious individual with a high level of proficiency in all aspects of modern warfare, especially regarding computer systems and electronic warfare.

He scores highly in marksmanship and unarmed combat and still holds the record for completing the Mobile Infantry Academy Assault Course in the shortest time.

His obvious competence can make him impatient with others he views as less capable but, on the positive side, this means he demands 100 per cent from the troopers under his command. Unfortunately, it can also make him headstrong and arrogant in situations where teamwork is required.

When extended to superior officers, this impatience rarely leads to outright insubordination, but Platoon Leader Costallion cites his 'reluctance to follow orders with which he personally disagrees' as one of the factors leading to delays in the recovery of the hostages at Constance Rigg – delays that may have caused otherwise preventable casualties.

Chapter 5
Aliss

The Doctor found himself in a large, echoing room. Judging by the empty cargo pallets, discarded spare parts, thick pipes running between floor and ceiling and racks of industrial equipment stacked against the walls, it had been designed as a storeroom. However, if the overturned plastic chairs, scattered plates and broken tables were anything to go by, it had been adapted for use as a communal area and canteen.

In the centre of the room, which was likely large enough to accommodate the base's entire complement of personnel, sat a young woman on a scuffed metal crate, staring at him with wide, terrified eyes.

The Doctor wasn't always very good at guessing people's ages but, if she were human, he thought she would be in her mid-to-late twenties.

Like many of the corpses outside, she wore a pair of orange work trousers and standard-issue trainers.

However, unlike the rest, she had a grubby chef's jacket over her T-shirt. She had wrapped her right wrist and forearm in a makeshift, grimy bandage. Her hair had once been tied back in a tidy ponytail, but now enough of it had come loose to frame her grime-smudged face with straggling curls.

The floor around her was clear of debris. A chunky laser pistol lay on the deck around ten feet from where she sat, as if she'd tossed it aside.

A little further from her, on the edge of the halo of broken furniture, lay another woman's body.

The Doctor heard Belinda step through the hatch behind him, followed by Shaya and all but two of her troopers, who'd been left outside to guard their backs.

The troopers kept their guns raised, pointing directly at the young woman, as they fanned out into a semicircle along the wall, keeping a tense and wary distance until they'd decided whether or not she posed a threat.

The Doctor tried to smile kindly at the woman, to put her at ease. Responding, she raised a hesitant hand, and began to sign as she spoke.

'Can you take me home?'

'We can do whatever you want,' the Doctor replied, also using sign language as well as speech. He took a step forwards.

'Do not approach!' Shaya ordered.

'Doctor, be careful,' said Belinda.

He paused. His first instinct had been to help this young woman, but perhaps a little caution was wise until he was certain what they were dealing with here. Whoever she was, this woman was the only survivor of a massacre, which meant she was almost certainly traumatised, and quite possibly responsible for at least some of the carnage.

'I've got a daughter,' the woman said desperately, still signing as she spoke. 'On Monpasso. She's with her grandad. She's two years old. I just want to see her.' Her eyes crept over to the dead body on the deck. 'And I shot Sal,' she admitted sadly. 'All right, I did it. But she was going to kill me.'

Cassio stepped forwards. He tapped a small square circuit on his armour and a hologram frame appeared in front of his left shoulder.

'You,' he said. As he spoke, the word 'YOU' appeared within the frame, and then scrolled upwards to make room for more words as he continued. 'Do not move. Eyes on me at all times, is that understood?'

The woman had been reading the captions as they appeared, and she nodded. 'Yes,' she said.

Gun raised, Cassio moved towards her, one step at a time, holding her stare. When he reached the laser gun, he bent slowly, not breaking her gaze, and retrieved it, before retreating back to the edge of the room.

The troopers seemed to relax slightly at the removal of the weapon from the woman's reach, but only slightly. The atmosphere in the room remained hair-trigger tense.

The Doctor caught her eye and, signing and speaking, asked, 'Who are you?'

'My name is Aliss Fenly,' she replied. 'And I just want to go home.'

Mo Gilliben consulted her scanner. 'Confirmed on the manifest,' she reported. 'Aliss Pabba Fenly, aged 28. Citizen of Monpasso. One daughter, Pelody.'

This time, the Doctor didn't bother to speak aloud, content to let his fingers do the talking.

Don't be scared, he signed.

You've all got guns, Aliss signed back, which he had to concede was a fair point. Having a squad of scared-looking troopers aim their rifles at you would be enough to make anyone nervous.

No, he gestured. *I don't. Trust me.*

Aliss smiled. *Thank you.*

With a snort of annoyance, Platoon Leader Shaya Costallion tapped her armour to activate her own subtitle hologram. 'I need you to keep everything audible,' she said. 'No private conversations.'

The Doctor sighed. 'Okay, gotcha.' He held out a hand to Trooper 7, who passed him a circuit square, which he clipped onto the breast of his suit.

'Doesn't matter what year it is, signing still makes some people paranoid.' He tapped the circuit square and a frame appeared by his chest. 'Hi there,' he said, signing with his fingers as his words appeared on the holo. 'My name is the Doctor.'

Aliss looked confused. 'I don't need a doctor. I just want to get home.'

Shaya stepped forwards. 'Tell us exactly what happened, Aliss.' Her words scrolled over her holo frame. 'Why did you kill that woman?'

Aliss swallowed. 'They all went mad. You've seen this place.' She glanced around at the strewn, splintered furniture. 'Every single person just went mad. It all happened so quickly.'

'But not you?' the Doctor asked.

Aliss let her shoulders slump. 'I don't know.' She glanced at the corpse. 'But that's Sal. She was my friend, and she was going to kill me with her bare hands. I've never fired a gun in my life, but what else could I do? I'm just the cook!' She looked on the verge of tears. 'I've been here for twelve months. I cook for them, that's all. It's not even real cooking, I just open flat-pack protein and add salt. That's all I do, every single day, and I had to kill my best friend.'

'Are you hurt?' Belinda asked. 'I'm sorry, I don't know how to sign, but …' She pointed to her wrist. 'Your arm. Does it hurt?'

Aliss seemed to understand. She looked down at her bandaged arm. 'I was running and I fell,' she said and signed. 'Everyone was panicking, and ...' She trailed off, swallowing hard.

Belinda stepped forwards. 'Can I take a look?'

'Do not approach!' Shaya ordered.

The Doctor gave her a withering look. 'Aw, come on.' He held out his hand again, and Trooper 7 gave him another circuit square, which he passed to Belinda.

'Do I just clip it on?' she asked.

'Yep.' The Doctor helped her fasten it in place. 'There you go. Now, just talk.'

Belinda knelt before Aliss, gently took her injured arm and began unwrapping it. 'It's okay,' she said, and the words scrolled across her holo-screen. 'I'm a nurse.'

Aliss's eyebrows shot up. 'A nurse who can't sign? That's against the law.'

'Right.' Belinda agreed. 'We have different laws where I come from, but it should be.'

The Doctor knelt beside Belinda.

'Aliss,' he said, 'can I ask? You've been on your own for a long time?'

Aliss gave a tight little nod. 'Fifteen days.'

'Do you know what it was, Aliss?' He gestured at the base around them. 'They all went crazy. Was there a noise, or a gas?' He remembered what Shaya

62

had told him as they approached the installation. 'The mineshaft operates as a mercury drop. Did any of the mercury escape, or …?'

Aliss shook her head, looking upset. 'I don't know.'

'Why did they smash all the mirrors?' the Doctor continued.

This time, Aliss didn't bother to speak. She touched the fingertips of her free hand to her forehead. *I don't know*. She started to cry.

Overcome with sympathy, the Doctor reached out and pulled her into a hug. Whatever else had happened, this poor girl had been locked in here alone for more than two weeks, with only the dead body of her best friend for company. She must have been so lonely and so frightened.

At first, she was stiff in his arms. She had been holding herself together for so long. But then she surrendered to the feeling of being hugged and comforted, the simple act of physical contact that let her know she wasn't alone any more. The Doctor felt her let go, and she started to sob into his shoulder. Loud, unselfconscious sobs like those of a child, howling out all the pain and fear of the past fifteen days.

Belinda sat back to give them space and turned to Mo. 'Is there a medical pack or something?' she whispered.

Mo nodded and went looking.

At the edge of the room, rifle still held ready, Cassio looked like he might explode. He turned off his holo-display and glared at his commanding officer. 'So we just abandon all protocol, is that it, ma'am?'

Shaya lowered her pistol. 'She doesn't look like she could break the necks of half the crew.'

'You hope.' Cassio's face hardened. 'And hope is irrelevant.'

'Okay.' Shaya decided to let his impersonation of her pass. She called out: 'Doctor, we need to get to Central Control. Stay here if you want—'

The Doctor disengaged from Aliss and turned with a sparkle of excitement in his eye. 'Ooh, gotta see that!' He signed to Aliss. 'I won't be long. Belinda's got you.'

Then he tapped his holo off and said, 'Bel, be careful of her, okay?'

Aliss gave him a look. 'I can still lip-read, you know.'

The Doctor grimaced. 'Right.' He signed, *Sorry.* Then he headed back towards Shaya.

'Troopers 2 and 6,' Shaya ordered, 'stay on guard here. Troopers 4 and 5, clear the body. Troopers 8 and 9, run a sweep of the hallways and check for any other survivors. And all of you, maintain a fifteen-foot radius around Aliss Fenly at all times.'

Beside her, Cassio scowled at Aliss. He tapped his holo, making sure it was on, so that when he spoke, she could read his words.

'Any sign of trouble,' he said, 'shoot to kill.'

Belinda wished the Doctor hadn't left her behind, but she knew she had to concentrate on her patient.

Mo came back with the base's medical kit, knelt beside Belinda and opened it up.

'Sorry,' she said. 'It's only a basic pack.'

Belinda considered the array of futuristic tools and gadgets and made a face. 'Um, thanks. But I don't know what any of this stuff does.'

Mo gave her a curious look. 'You're a funny sort of nurse.'

'It has been said.' Belinda smiled. There was something reassuring in the fact that Mo was the same age she was. The other soldiers, who were standing warily by the wall, were closed-mouthed and intimidating, but Mo talked to her with the openness of a friend.

Belinda began to rummage through the kit, searching for something familiar. 'Still, it's common sense,' she muttered. Even here in the far future, some things were still the same. 'Swabs, bandages …' She recognised something from treating the injured on Missbelindachandra One. 'Oh, that's simolin!'

She turned back to Aliss and tapped her chest, making sure her holo was on. 'It's just a graze. I can clean it up and stop it stinging.' Belinda gave her best reassuring bedside smile. 'I know you've had a terrible time, but we're gonna do everything to help.'

Aliss had recovered her composure. Weeping into the Doctor's hug seemed to have released an inner tension. She looked exhausted. 'That's so kind of you,' she said.

Belinda turned back to the kit, and she and Mo began to sort out what they were going to need.

Behind them, Aliss slid her gaze to the right and terror passed across her face. She flicked her eyes forwards again before anyone could catch her looking off to the side.

It was still there, still behind her.

After all this time, all this death, the presence was still there, just beyond the edge of her peripheral vision.

Waiting …

PERSONNEL FILE

NAME: Kai Sabba
RANK: Trooper
AGE: 25
PLACE OF BIRTH: Onn-far Agri-District

PROFILE
A talented scout and tracker, Sabba was recruited into Forward Reconnaissance, where he quickly distinguished himself, locating and neutralising an enemy command bunker during the Siege of Snowy Peaks and preventing his entire squad from walking into a razor-minefield on Valak-6, at the cost of his own leg.

Sabba was also instrumental in the tracking and apprehension of Commander Eli Dortmann and his unit when they went rogue during the final days of the Assault on Great Glacier Valley.

ASSESSMENT

Sabba's formidable tracking skills have proven an asset to his team during operations and manhunts throughout Sector Eighteen. What he lacks in combat experience, he makes up for in dedication and a willingness to follow orders.

As the youngest of three brothers (all deceased) he tends to hero-worship older male members of his team, such as Cassio Palin-Paleen – but as this tendency drives him to emulate their achievements and rise to their standards, this is no bad thing.

Given the right encouragement and training, he may one day rise to lead his own platoon.

Chapter 6
Where No Light Has Ever Been

The Doctor held back while Shaya and Cassio entered the room first, guns raised.

After a moment, Shaya called, 'All clear. Safe to proceed,' and the Doctor and Trooper 7 joined them.

The Central Control Room, as its name suggested, had been the heart of the mining operation. It was a large, equipment-filled chamber with a deep well at the centre. Huge and heavy mining apparatus stood suspended over it.

Above the well, a platform held workstations and instrument panels, with enough screens, dials and switches to excite the Doctor's curiosity.

Once, this had been a busy hub of activity. Now it was silent and abandoned.

Shaya and Cassio went for the controls, attempting to reactivate them in order to find out what had happened there. Trooper 7 stayed on guard by the door, but the Doctor strode straight to the edge of the hole. He couldn't help himself.

'No bodies,' he said, looking around the floor. 'Maybe they ran from this place first.' Which meant this was where the trouble had started. 'Nice thought!'

He leant over the edge of the hole and looked down. The walls of the shaft went down a long way, eventually vanishing into darkness.

'So, what, is this the seed-well?' he asked.

Shaya glanced up from her instruments. 'That's where they first dropped the mercury lines and drilled down. Capable of hauling up two blades of carbon 46, every day.'

Carbon-46 . . . She'd mentioned that before, the Doctor realised. It was not a designation he was familiar with. But words, minerals, nothing seemed to matter much as he stared into the absolute darkness of that apparently bottomless hole.

A memory tickled him. An early incident from one of his past lives, millennia ago, when he'd peered down another such hole. The Daleks had drilled that one in an attempt to destroy the Earth's molten core, but that had all happened a long time ago, when Susan was still with him, and he'd been much older back then . . .

'Hello …' he called, hoping for an echo. There was only silence. He shrugged, and looked up at Shaya. 'No one home.'

Her lips twitched with a smile she tried to hide from Cassio, and the Doctor grinned back.

He moved around the edge of the hole, loving the thrill of standing on the lip of such a spectacular drop. 'A well, five miles deep,' he marvelled, balancing on the edge of the abyss. 'Beneath the planet's crust, where no light has ever been before.'

He wondered how long it would take to fall that far. In standard Earth mavity (and this felt fairly close), a falling person would reach terminal velocity within the first twelve seconds of their drop. After that, they'd fall at around 120 miles per hour. That meant a fall of five miles would take approximately two-and-a-half minutes.

Not that you'd likely be conscious all that time. Falling at that speed, the frontal lobes of your brain would be starved of oxygen, which meant you'd pass out after a minute or so. Although that would probably be the longest and simultaneously shortest minute of your life.

Time to think about your loved ones and regret the decisions that had led you to be plummeting into the depths of the planet, but not enough time to boil an egg or finish a crossword.

'Nothing's responding,' Shaya cursed. 'Someone's put a good old-fashioned restraining bolt on the system …' She glanced around and then pointed. 'There!'

High above them, among the mining equipment suspended from the ceiling, unknown hands had bolted a knot of cables and pipes to the side of the main drill. With a determined look on her face, she pulled out her pistol and took aim.

'Whoa!' the Doctor called in alarm. 'Don't hit the roof!'

'Careful, boss,' Cassio murmured.

Shaya didn't blink. Her finger tightened on the trigger and a single shot rang out, loud in the confined space.

A perfect hit.

Severed cables swung free. The lights flickered on, and all the controls came to life.

The Doctor was impressed. 'Good shot.'

Shaya holstered her weapon. 'I was brought up in the Wildlands,' she said. 'Shooting drought-sharks from the age of six. I could run faster than a snake-lighter. That's how I got into the forces. At fourteen years old.'

Fourteen? 'That's a bit young,' the Doctor said.

Shaya shrugged. 'The fight began the day I was born. I'm a citizen of Lombardo.'

'Oh.' The Doctor had heard of Lombardo. 'Tough place. Brutal.' A sudden thought struck him. 'So, in this century, Lombardo's in a joint foundation with Earth, right? Belinda's from Earth.'

Shaya's face registered only puzzlement. 'From where?'

'Planet Earth.'

'Never heard of it.'

Hunched over a keyboard, Cassio gave a grunt. 'Stupid name for a planet.'

'But the human race?' The Doctor thought maybe they'd misunderstood somehow. 'You've heard of that?'

Shaya shook her head. 'Not in these parts.'

He began to feel uneasy. 'But Earth's part of the foundation, right now. That's a fact.'

She gave him a look. 'Your tests are very strange.' Then she turned to Cassio. 'Okay, let's see if you can revive the base log stats and index file. Let's find out what happened here.'

They got to work, tapping at keyboards, but the Doctor remained where he was, standing at the edge of the well.

Earth and Lombardo were supposed to be allies in this time period. If these two had never even *heard* of Earth, then something had gone terribly wrong with history.

It was as if, somehow, the Earth had stopped existing.

Having cleared away Sal's body, the troopers were sitting with their backs to the wall in the main hall, eating from their wafer packs.

Keeping the mandated distance of fifteen feet from Aliss, Belinda and Mo were kneeling over the medical kit, preparing a dish of paste.

'It was bad luck, me and the Doctor coming along,' Belinda said. 'Cos you're a squad of eleven, and we made it thirteen.'

Mo gave her a quizzical glance. 'You both say such funny things. What does that mean?'

'What does ...?' Belinda blinked in surprise. 'Has that gone? Thirteen as unlucky?' she asked. 'Is that an old Earth thing?'

This time, Mo frowned in genuine confusion. 'An old what thing?'

'Earth? The human race?'

'What's that, then?'

Belinda couldn't believe it. 'Have you ever heard of planet Earth?'

As she spoke, she looked across at Aliss. And just for a second, she thought she saw –

'Oh!'

'What?' Mo asked.

Belinda shook her head. Her eyes were playing tricks on her. 'Nothing.' She tapped her holo frame, so that Aliss would know what they were saying. 'Sorry. I just thought …'

Mo looked back and forth from Belinda to Aliss. 'What is it?'

By the wall, Kai got to his feet, suddenly alert. 'What is it?' he asked. 'What happened?'

Belinda turned off her holo display, to hide her words from Aliss. 'Nothing. I just thought I saw …'

She stood up, and keeping the required fifteen feet from where Aliss sat, she began to walk around the edge of the room. 'I'm getting paranoid,' she joked.

Kai didn't laugh. 'What did you see?'

'I didn't.'

Holding his rifle ready, Kai began to circle the room in the opposite direction. 'Anyone there?' he shouted.

The room was clearly empty. Belinda said, 'Honestly, there's nothing. It was just me.' She tapped her holo back on and turned so Aliss could read it. 'I'm sorry,' she said, feeling foolish. 'I'm being mad.'

Aliss raised her hand. 'I want to go home,' she said, signing emphatically.

Of course she did. After everything this poor girl had been through, the last thing she needed was for her nurse to start getting spooked by things that weren't there.

Belinda felt her cheeks grow hot. To cover her embarrassment, she turned to Mo. 'Is it ready yet?'

Mo looked up. 'Yup!' She handed over the bowl. 'Just paste that on.' She grinned. 'Here I am, teaching the nursing staff.'

Belinda returned her smile. 'You're amazing. Thanks, Mo.' She walked over to Aliss and tapped her holo projector. 'Okay, I'm just going to paste this on the wound.'

Aliss nodded and held out her injured arm. Using a spatula, Belinda began to carefully apply the mixture, making sure it covered every part of the graze. After two weeks wrapped in a filthy bandage, the skin had started to become infected, and Belinda wanted to make sure she treated it all.

As she worked, Belinda talked. It was an old habit she'd picked up in the hospital, chatting away to put patients at their ease and distract them from their injuries while she treated them. As she spoke, her holo display translated her words into text for Aliss.

'I was saying, about the traditions of the human race.'

Aliss gave her a blank look.

'Have you ever met any?' Belinda asked. 'Humans, I mean?'

Aliss shook her head. 'I've never heard of you.'

PERSONNEL FILE

NAME: Mo Gilliben
RANK: Trooper
AGE: 26
PLACE OF BIRTH: Malla Forge
Industrial Zone

PROFILE

Gilliben joined Forward Reconnaissance straight from Basic Training, where she demonstrated a particular aptitude for search-and-rescue. Since then, she has acquitted herself satisfactorily during several high-profile recovery missions, including the location and release of 24 hostages held by the Red Tree

Alliance and the rescue of the crew and passengers of the civilian transport Scarlet Maiden, which lost power close to the Frellian Singularity. The transport would have been sucked in and destroyed if not for the efforts of Gilliben and her commanding officer, Platoon Leader Costallion.

ASSESSMENT

While she has not yet engaged in direct combat, Gilliben's training scores indicate her to be an exceptionally capable recruit, even if her enthusiasm and outgoing nature can sometimes make her appear gauche. She has an exceptional working relationship with Costallion.

Chapter 7
This is How it Started

The Doctor watched as Cassio worked at the reactivated controls. The soldier was trying to access the security footage from inside the base in the lead-up to the massacre but, frustratingly, the screens showed nothing but static.

'They wiped all the video-chains,' he said. 'Why would they do that? Everything's been erased.'

The Doctor pulled his sonic screwdriver from one of his suit's equipment pouches. 'Everything's been restored,' he announced grandly, and jammed the device into the controls.

The screens blinked and flickered, and pictures resolved out of the chaos, complete with scrolling info text and company logos.

Shaya looked at the sonic. 'What is that thing?'

The Doctor's eyes twinkled. 'Magic.'

He wasn't being entirely facetious. Arthur C. Clarke, the British author and inventor of the communication satellite, had famously once written, 'Any sufficiently advanced technology is indistinguishable from magic.' Compared to the tech Shaya and Cassio were used to, Time Lord devices were very, very advanced. If he tried to explain that the sonic worked via a psychic connection that fed his wishes through an internal computational matrix the size of a planet yet encased in something no larger than a mobile phone, they wouldn't understand. For now, it was enough that it worked – so magic it was.

To Cassio, he said, 'Try to find the last entry.'

The soldier clenched his jaw and looked to Shaya. 'Platoon Leader, does this "Doctor" have authority over me?'

'Right now, he does,' she replied, 'yes.'

Fuming, Cassio stabbed at the controls with his fingers. Images and text flickered across the screens. 'It's still corrupted,' he said. 'We've got fragments.'

The images stopped.

'Hold on.' Cassio spooled them backwards until – 'Here it is, the Base Commander's final statement …'

The screens filled with light and noise. A tough-looking middle-aged man stared wide-eyed into a handheld camera. The info text identified him as Ulric Dazen. Beside him stood Sal, the woman Aliss had killed, and behind them, people were running and shouting in terror.

'It's behind you,' Ulric was saying. 'It is behind you!'

'It came from the Well!' Sal interrupted. They were yelling over each other.

'That's what it does!'

'It came out of the Well!'

'It's always behind you!'

'And we don't know how to stop it!'

The images cut out.

The Doctor looked around the control room. That footage had been shot right here, fifteen days ago. But now there weren't even any bodies here. They'd fled this room before they died.

Shaya and Cassio looked stunned. This was obviously far worse than either of them had been prepared for.

For a moment, the three of them stood in silence, each wrapped in their own thoughts.

Then, 'Ma'am.'

They jumped, and turned to find Troopers 8 and 9 at the doorway.

'Not now,' Shaya snapped. 'Thank you.'

Trooper 9 turned to leave, but 8 hesitated. 'It's just, we checked the walkways and found the rest of them dead. Every member of the Base's crew. Which confirms that Aliss Fenly is the only one left alive.'

The Doctor put a hand to his chin. 'So the one who survived is deaf.'

Cassio gave him a look that was equal parts scorn and fear. 'Is that important?'

The Doctor raised an eyebrow. 'I don't know. Is it?'

Once she had applied the paste to Aliss's graze, Belinda began to wrap the arm with a fresh bandage. Behind her, having returned from disposing of Sal's body, Troopers 5 and 6 rejoined Trooper 4 to eat their rations. Kai stayed where he was, a few paces further around the edge of the room than the others, still watchful.

'It's so strange,' Belinda said. 'Cos the Doctor said – and hey, I should mention, I hardly know him, okay? Isn't that strange? But he's the expert – he said to me, everyone's heard of—' She glanced up at Aliss. 'Oh!'

Shocked, Belinda fell back. For a second, for *half* a second, a *millisecond*, she had seen a shape. Not really a shape, even. The edge of something.

The hint of the edge of … *something*.

Almost as if someone had been standing directly behind Aliss and had peeked out for the briefest instant. Then a blur and it was gone.

'What?' Aliss asked innocently. 'What is it? What? What happened?'

The troopers were all on their feet now, alarmed.

'What is it?' Kai demanded. 'What did she do?'

'No, but she didn't.' Belinda swallowed. She stood up and tried to compose herself. She tapped the holo off. 'I'm stupid, there's nothing there. I'm sorry.'

She looked around Aliss and there was clearly no one hiding. The room was large and empty and echoing. Nobody could be there without being seen. And yet, just for that instant . . .

'Yeah, but that's twice,' Mo said. 'What did you see?'

Fearfully, Aliss looked between them. They both had their holos off and had turned away from her so she couldn't read their lips. 'Please?' she asked. 'Please can you tell me what you're saying?'

Belinda reactivated her display. 'I'm sorry, I didn't mean to scare you, Aliss. I just . . . I thought I saw something behind you.'

Aliss blinked in surprise. She looked around. 'Well, there isn't anything, is there?' She held up her arms. 'And look at me. All clean.'

She began to turn on the spot and Belinda couldn't help feeling a stab of irrational fright. But no, there was nothing lurking behind her. She was just a woman turning on the spot with her arms in the air. Perfectly normal, nothing to see.

Belinda sighed. 'I'm sorry. It's just me.'

Kai was still suspicious. 'What did it look like?'

'It didn't. It's an empty room. There's no one there.'

'You thought you saw a *person*?' Mo asked.

'Yes, but I didn't, did I?' Belinda was getting flustered now, torn between what she thought she'd seen and what she knew was impossible. She noticed the bandage she'd been tying, now lying heaped on the floor beside the crate, and sighed. 'Now, I've got this dirty.' She picked it up and went back to the med kit for a clean one.

'All the same.' Kai raised his gun at Aliss. Mo and the other troopers watched closely, guns ready, but not aiming yet. Kai tapped on his holo display. 'Stay where you are, Aliss Fenly.'

Aliss looked around and flapped her arms in an exasperated shrug. 'Where exactly am I going to go?'

'Keep it calm,' Kai warned, voice tight with tension. 'Thank you.' He stared at her, eyes locked, almost daring her to make a move.

Then, his brow twitched almost imperceptibly. He tilted his head to one side and his gaze flicked to the left side of her face …

'What?' Aliss said.

'Nothing.'

Belinda heard the uncertainty in his tone. 'Did you see something?' she asked.

'No.'

'Then, what was it?'

'Nothing.'

'Oh, for heaven's sake,' Mo said. 'It's a great big empty room. There can't be anything, can there?' She walked around the edge of the room until she was almost opposite Kai. 'Aliss?' she said. Then, realising she was out of Aliss's eyeline, 'Oh, sorry.' She double-tapped the circuit square. 'Cast to Trooper 2.' Then, connection established, she gave a single tap and said, 'Aliss, turn to your right.'

ALISS TURN TO YOUR RIGHT appeared on Kai's display.

Aliss read it and scowled resentfully. She scooted around to face Mo. 'I don't know what you're trying to prove.'

Belinda wished she'd never started any of this. She'd made a mistake and now everybody was jumpy and freaking out and scaring the hell out of a poor, traumatised woman.

'Leave her alone, Mo. Come on.'

Mo clenched her jaw. 'No, but ...' She paused and frowned. And then slowly, carefully, leant to her left. 'Whoa!' Her head jerked back and her eyes were wide.

Across the room, Kai looked on the verge of panic. 'But there's nothing,' he protested. 'Look, I can see. There's not anything. There's literally nothing!'

'But I saw something,' Mo insisted. 'And you saw it before. You did, you saw it.'

'But there's nothing there!'

Aliss stood up. 'I know what you're saying!' She looked from one to the other. 'And I've seen this before. This is how it started, and this is how I ended up killing my friend before she killed me. There is absolutely nothing there. There is nothing behind me. *Nothing!*'

Kai activated his holo display. 'Okay,' he said. 'Let's prove it.' He kept his gun trained on Aliss, so she would keep looking at him, and moved back to the door.

'Hanno,' he said, addressing Trooper 4. 'Hanno, I'll keep guard here. I want you to establish Aliss Fenly as your centre point and execute a complete circle of the room.'

Hanno gave a nod, and began moving around the perimeter, stepping around and over bits of broken furniture.

Aliss began to cry. 'Please, leave me alone.'

'Look at her,' Belinda said to Kai. 'She's terrified.'

Kai turned off his display. Keeping his eyes fixed on Aliss, he spoke from the corner of his mouth.

'You. Will be. Quiet. Or you will be considered a threat to life.'

Mo put a hand on Belinda's arm and pulled her back, away from the confrontation.

Reactivating the display, Kai addressed Aliss. 'You will stay looking at me. Do not look away. Hanno, execute the move.'

And Hanno, her gun also raised, continued walking in an arc, moving slowly, one step at a time …

PERSONNEL FILE

NAME:	Hanno Yeft
RANK:	Trooper
AGE:	28
PLACE OF BIRTH:	The Violet Forest
	Panambra

PROFILE

Yeft was born on her parents' freighter during a stopover on Panambra in the Weylion Expanse.

The family owned and ran a transport business, ferrying passengers and cargo between worlds in the Outer Colonies. Yeft expected to inherit the business when her parents died.

However, following the surprise attacks at Misenfold and the Katari Decandencia, she followed her brother into the military.

She served under General Chinchappa during the Quelling of the Silver Tongues and the Sontaran Incursion, and took part in the successful campaign to liberate Panambra from the Merciful Swarm Hegemony.

Her enlistment to Costallion's Forward Reconnaissance team was suggested by Cassio Palin-Paleen, who completed his Basic Training with Yeft's brother, Janno Yeft (MIA at the Battle of Sawtooth Ridge) and seems to have assumed some sort of responsibility for his friend's younger sister.

ASSESSMENT
Yeft's upbringing on a merchant freighter instilled in her a powerful sense of teamwork and discipline, making her eminently suited to a career in the military. However, while she is an exemplary soldier, she shows little personal initiative and her prospects for promotion are small.

Chapter 8
Carbon-46

The Doctor leant over the back of Cassio's chair as the soldier analysed the fragment of footage they'd just watched. Desperate to glean as much information as possible, they had run it backwards and forwards, slow and fast.

Now, the Doctor's finger jabbed at the screen.

'Him.' In the background, a man was yelling in Ulric's direction, but the words were lost in the hubbub. 'Isolate him.'

Cassio's fingers rattled on the keyboard, and the image zoomed in, pixels bristling.

The face was that of the first corpse the group had discovered upon entering the base. The info text identified him as Chief Engineer Albie Bethick.

He was plainly terrified.

'Can we isolate his sound?' the Doctor asked.

Cassio shook his head. 'No coverage. He's too deep, too far from the microphone.'

The Doctor rolled his eyes, leant over and tapped the controls, ignoring the soldier's protests. The background noise dulled. Now, Bethick's shouted words were distorted, but just about audible.

'We don't know what it is!' he kept repeating. 'We don't know what it is! *We don't know what it is!*'

The clip ended. Shaya and Cassio looked chilled, but the Doctor's mind whirled.

Somewhere in there, old memories stirred.

'We don't know what it is.' He made a face. Whatever had attacked these people, they hadn't been able to identify it. It had been something they'd never seen before.

And that made sense. Nothing familiar could live in a place like this, entirely inimical to unprotected life.

'Like …'

A memory started to rise – one he'd been trying very hard to keep buried. He turned and walked a few paces. Touched a finger to his lower lip. 'Oh my old, old head. This planet is flooded with Galvanic Radiation. But where's it from?'

'Well, the sun.' Shaya straightened up. 'But it's just a Grey Star now. Nothing special.'

The Doctor wouldn't be put off. He was close to something, he just knew it. He could feel a dark cloud of apprehension building like a thunderhead.

'But a Grey Star is a star that's collapsed. What was it before?'

'It was an Xtonic Star,' Shaya said, clearly wondering if this was still part of a test. 'But that's ancient history, from 400,000 years ago. The sun burned out and the wars came. They stripped all the carbon off the surface of this planet and left it ruined.'

'When you say carbon ...'

'Carbon-46.'

The Doctor realised he'd never got round to asking what Carbon-46 was. 'And the definition of that is ...?'

'Diamonds.' Shaya shrugged. 'This is a diamond mine. The entire surface of this planet was once made out of diamonds. They're just stripping out the last subterranean seams.'

The Doctor froze then turned slowly to face her.

'... *what?*'

In the main hall, Belinda and Mo watched Hanno continue to step carefully around the circumference of the room, navigating pieces of strewn equipment and broken plastic furniture. By the door, Kai had his gun aimed at Aliss, and she was crying.

'Please stop,' she whispered hoarsely.

'Or what?' Kai asked.

And Hanno took another step …

'What's the name of the planet?' the Doctor demanded.

Please, please don't let it be the one I think it is.

Anything but that …

'6-7-6-7,' Shaya said.

'No, no, no.' He banged the heel of his hand against his forehead. 'The old name.' He felt like a cartoon character that had run off a cliff but hadn't fallen yet because he hadn't looked down. 'What was it called 400,000 years ago?'

'Don't,' warned Aliss, still facing Kai.

Kai ignored her. From his vantage point, Hanno was almost completely behind her now.

Just two more steps, and she'd be completely hidden from him.

He had eyes on Belinda and Mo, still standing by the med kit. The other troopers were spread out in a fan to either side of him. Everyone was watching. Once Hanno passed completely behind Aliss, she would be covering his blind spot on the far side of the room, leaving nowhere for anyone or anything to hide.

He'd done what he thought Cassio would have done in the same position, and he hoped the second-in-command would be proud of him.

'Please, don't,' Aliss said again, but she sounded defeated now.

Hanno took one more step.

The Doctor waited while Shaya consulted her scanner, flicking back through the mission briefing until she found the information, buried in an appendix at the end.

'It was called Midnight.'

No! The Doctor put a hand to his mouth. He could feel both his heartbeats thumping in his ears. *No, no, no, no ...*

Not that. Not the greatest terror he'd ever experienced. Not again.

Shaya looked up from her scanner. 'What? What is it?'

The Doctor squeezed his eyes tight shut and clenched his fists until his nails dug into his palms.

'I've been here before,' he said.

And he turned and ran.

Hanno took the last step. Now, from Kai's point of view, she was completely hidden behind Aliss.

This will prove it, Kai thought. *There's nothing there. Nowhere to hide. We can stop this nonsense –*

Hanno screamed and flew through the air, thrown like a doll.

At first, Kai thought she'd stepped on a landmine, then he realised there hadn't been an explosion. Hanno travelled twenty feet across the room and crashed into a glass hydroponics case, shattering the glass and landing among the plants with a heavy thud and a loud clatter of equipment.

Everyone shouted at once. The other troopers scrambled to bring their weapons to bear.

'What did you do?' Kai jabbed his gun at Aliss. 'What did you do?'

'It wasn't me. I didn't do anything!'

'She was just sitting there!' Belinda shouted.

'She didn't even move!' Mo agreed.

Kai's knuckle tensed on the trigger. As far as he was concerned, his squad was under attack, and he had to defend it.

Before Kai could nerve himself to fire, the Doctor burst into the room. 'Stop, stop, stop, stop, stop!' He held up his hands, urging them all back. 'Don't go near her. Step back, step back.' He took a breath. 'Now, what happened?'

'She threw her across the room,' Mo said, pointing to Aliss. She ducked around him and ran to where Hanno lay.

'No,' Belinda yelled. She wanted to help, too, but she knew Hanno couldn't have survived that impact. 'Mo, don't. Come back!'

The Doctor turned to face Aliss, who was watching them all with frightened, tear-reddened eyes.

'What did you do?' he asked, making sure his holo displayed the words for her.

'It wasn't me,' she protested.

'It wasn't her,' Belinda agreed, grabbing his sleeve. 'Mo,' she called, 'come back over here. Listen to me, come back.'

Being careful of the broken glass, Mo reached down and put her fingers to the side of Hanno's throat. Then she stood up with a grim expression. 'She's dead.'

'Just come back,' Belinda urged. 'Don't go behind Aliss. Don't go *anywhere* behind her. Don't you see?'

Obviously frightened, Mo nodded, and hurried back, skirting around the edge of the room.

'What do you mean?' the Doctor asked.

Belinda gripped his arm, scarcely able to believe what she was saying. 'There's something behind her.'

Shaya and the rest of the squad came in.

'What's happened?' the patrol leader demanded, immediately taking control of the situation. 'Everyone, stay where you are. Report, Trooper 2.'

Kai lowered his gun. 'I don't know, ma'am. I don't know what happened, she just got … thrown.'

Cassio looked across the room, to where Hanno lay in the ruins of the glass hydroponics case. 'Is she dead?' His expression tightened. 'I trained with her brother.'

'Yes, she's dead,' Mo said, visibly upset. 'I'm so sorry. It just happened, it was so fast.'

Cassio made a gesture and the other troopers began to spread out around the walls of the room, forming a rough semicircle with Aliss as its central focus.

'Did you do this?' Cassio demanded.

'Just try to stay calm,' the Doctor urged.

'I do not take orders from you!' Cassio snapped back, whirling to point his gun at the Doctor.

The Doctor held up his palms in a gesture of surrender and, point made, Cassio turned back to Aliss. He raised the muzzle of his rifle until it was aimed directly at her forehead. With a slap, he activated his holo display. 'Did you kill her?'

'No!' she insisted.

'Then who did?'

For a long instant, they glared at each other. Then something inside Aliss seemed to snap.

'There's something behind me,' she shouted, signing furiously. 'All right? There is something. Behind me! I don't know what it is, no one knows what it is. It can't be seen and it can't be stopped, but there's something behind me *all the time!* Now, please. Help me.'

Silence followed this outburst. Even Cassio took a step back.

The Doctor made sure his holo display was lit. 'Aliss,' he said gently. 'Explain. What do you mean?'

Aliss looked suddenly exhausted. She had unburdened herself of the secret she'd been carrying, but had been left only with the hopelessness of someone who'd already played out this scene before, and hadn't liked how it ended.

'Something came out of the Well. That's what they said.' Tired and edgy, she rubbed her forehead. 'It came out of the Well, and they said it was laughing. And now they're all dead and it's behind me.'

The Doctor clicked his tongue. Of all the planets they could have fallen onto, of all the radioactive hellholes and war-ravaged badlands, they'd had to choose this one.

'Just look,' Belinda said. 'Look behind her. Please, all of you, just look.'

'It doesn't make any sense,' Shaya said. 'There can't be anything behind her. We can see her from every angle.' She began walking clockwise around the edge of the semicircle of troopers.

'Try telling *it* that,' Belinda said. 'And *look*.'

Shaya stopped. Her eyes narrowed.

They were all staring now. The troopers, the Doctor. Everyone.

Then, one by one, their heads tilted to the left.

There, behind Aliss …

A shadow?

A hint of something not *quite* visible?

'Can you see it?' Aliss asked, voice quavering.

No one answered. They were all frozen, unable to take their eyes from the merest sliver of a suggestion of a presence over her left shoulder.

Cassio was the first to shake himself free. 'No!' Obstinately, he thrust his chin and his weapon forwards. 'This is just an illusion. It has to be some kind of trick. Maybe there's gas, or poison. Hallucinogenic warfare. We saw what happened to the base. They went mad.'

'No, but hold on.' The Doctor held up a finger. 'Just listen.'

Cassio glared at Shaya. 'Permission to override the orders of this civilian, ma'am?'

Shaya looked thoughtfully at the Doctor. Out of everyone in this room, he seemed to be the only one with any semblance of understanding. From a tactical viewpoint, she'd rather understand what they were facing before she let Cassio and the other troopers off the leash – a scenario that would most likely involve the immediate execution of the only survivor of the installation's original crew, and the only witness who might be able to shed any light on the situation.

'Permission not given,' she barked. 'Now, listen to the Doctor.'

'No,' the Doctor said. 'Listen to Belinda!' He turned on his heel to face her. 'What did you mean, Bel? Why did you tell Mo not to go behind Aliss?'

Finding herself suddenly the focus of attention, Belinda swallowed. She was used to conveying vital information in emergency situations. And right now, somebody needed to take control of this mess. She figured it may as well be her.

She bent down and grabbed three rusty iron bolts from the debris on the floor. 'It's like this,' she said and placed one bolt back on the deck about a foot away. 'Imagine this is Aliss.' She placed the second bolt close to the toes of her boots. 'And this is us, facing her.' She glanced around to make sure everyone was following. 'Now, there is something behind her. And if *you* stand behind *it* …' She placed the third bolt down on the other side of the first, forming a straight line with the bolt representing Aliss as its midpoint. ' … you die.'

She slapped the third bolt, sending it rolling and clanging across the metal floor.

The Doctor's face looked like it was carved from stone. 'If that was a clockface,' he said, 'with Aliss in the middle and us at 6 o'clock, then … You die at midnight.'

Belinda stood back up, wiping grease from her hands. 'Well, that's what happened,' she said. 'That's what I saw. And that's why I'm telling you, stay back. Don't go behind her. Don't go directly behind her, or you're dead.'

Cassio's lip curled. 'In that case …' He marched

straight over to Aliss, and pressed his rifle barrel into her chest. 'If there's something behind you,' he snarled, 'then why don't we get rid of you?'

Aliss looked up at him with a mixture of fear and defiance. 'Because if you kill me,' she told him bitterly, 'it goes behind *you*.' She looked around at all the staring faces and gave a derisive snort. 'What? Did you think it went for me first? Do you think it crawled its way out of Hell just to get to little old me? You idiots. I'm *nothing*. I'm just the only one left.'

'Half of them broken,' Shaya said in sudden realisation. 'Half of them shot.'

Aliss gave her a contemptuous look. 'They killed each other to get rid of it. But if you kill the host, it jumps over to you. It hides behind your back, and it stays there for ever.'

'Cassio,' Shaya snapped. 'Step away.'

Cassio threw her an angry look, but Aliss clearly had him rattled. Furious but unnerved, he stepped back to join the others at the periphery of the semicircle.

'Doctor,' Shaya continued. 'You said you'd been here before. When was that?'

The Doctor gave a sigh. 'Different life. Back when it was a world made of diamonds.' His expression hardened as he delved into memories he'd been suppressing for five very long lifetimes. 'And I met something so … *vile*.'

Chapter 9
No Other Way

In his tenth incarnation, the Doctor had stopped here, on the planet Midnight, for a holiday. Back then, the diamond-covered world had played host to a luxury hotel. People had come from all over the galaxy to enjoy views of the unique crystal landscape. They couldn't stand outside because of the deadly galvanic radiation that saturated the surface, but they could admire the scenery through special windows made of toughened glass.

Of course, his companion, Donna Noble, had been more interested in sampling the spa treatments and restaurants on offer than gawking through the window at a load of precious stones she couldn't even touch. So, when he'd suggested a tourist excursion in a heavily shielded surface rover to see the Sapphire Waterfall, she hadn't been keen.

'A sapphire waterfall!' he'd protested. 'A waterfall, made of sapphires! This enormous jewel, the size of a glacier, reaches the Cliffs of Oblivion, and then shatters into sapphires at the edge, and they fall 100,000 feet into a crystal ravine.'

'I bet you say that to all the girls,' Donna replied.

'Oh, come on.' It was one of the wonders of the known universe. A sight many travelled thousands of light years to witness, and he was determined to see it even if Donna seemed unimpressed with the idea. 'They're boarding now, and it's no fun if I see it on my own. Four hours, that's all it takes.'

Donna scoffed. 'No, that's four hours there and four back. It's like a school trip. I'd rather go sunbathing.'

'You be careful,' he said. 'That's Xtonic sunlight.'

'Oh, I'm safe. It says in the brochure, this glass is fifteen feet thick.'

And so he'd given up trying to persuade her. He'd left her at the hotel and clambered aboard the heavy steel rover – a big space truck, he'd called it – with a handful of other sightseers, and settled in for the four-hour journey to the Falls.

Back then, there had only been the hotel on the planet. Nothing else. And before the Leisure Palace Company had dropped the pre-constructed building into place from orbit, no one had come here in all eternity. The planet had remained pristine and untouched, devoid of atmosphere *and life. Nothing could survive the galvanic radiation bombarding the surface from the Xtonic Star.*

At least, that's what they'd thought …

… Right up until the moment something started banging on the outside of the rover.

The Doctor faced Aliss so she could read his holo display as he spoke. 'It had no name, no face, no … self.' He gave a tight little shake of the head. 'And I have never been so scared in my life.'

'What did it do?' Belinda asked.

'It had fun.' He gave a bitter chuckle. 'Oh, it played games.'

Somehow, the nameless presence killed the drivers and found its way inside, where it possessed one of the passengers.

Maybe in her distressed state, Sky Silvestry had been the weakest, the one least able to keep it out of her head – or maybe she had simply been the first it reached.

The presence seemed childlike and uncomprehending, simply repeating what they said; a parrot mimicking sounds without understanding, or a child trying to annoy its older sibling.

But then a strange thing happened.

The delay between the Doctor speaking and the thing repeating his words started to shrink.

It had been studying him, and had begun to anticipate what he was about to say next. And eventually, after about fifteen minutes of further study, it was able to speak in complete unison with him, matching each and every syllable he uttered, however he tried to trick it.

And after that ...

'I think it was learning,' the Doctor said with a shudder. That thing had got inside his head. First it matched him, and then it started speaking before him, stole his words before he could verbalise them and left *him* as the one doing the repeating. It held him paralysed in its thrall, ripped hungrily through the attic of his memory, gathered strength from every fear and regret, every grief and anguish, until it had been on the verge of consuming him entirely. And he had been powerless to stop it. He had been entirely at its mercy, and the only reason he'd survived at all was because the rover's hostess, whose name he never even knew, sacrificed herself to drag the creature inhabiting Mrs Silvestry out, onto the surface, breaking the spell.

Even now, lifetimes later, he felt weak with fear at the thought of being so completely unable to move or speak, except to repeat the words the creature said. And he still shivered at the memory of the terrible coldness of its presence in his mind – a cold that sapped both his strength and his will.

Cassio sneered. 'You say you saw this 400,000 years ago?' He turned to Shaya. 'And you're listening to him?'

Shaya pursed her lips, and the Doctor could see she was starting to have doubts. 'He might have information,' she said uncertainly.

Cassio gave an exasperated snort and drew himself up. 'Then I'm declaring a Red Code.'

Shaya looked shocked. 'You can't do that!'

'This is exactly what a Red Code is for. When the leader is incompetent, the deputy takes over. Am I seconded?' No one spoke. He looked to the other troopers and shouted. 'Am I seconded?'

Kai gave a nod and stamped to attention. 'Yes, sir.'

Cassio gave a satisfied smirk. 'Then it's done. Until such time as we reach a disciplinary court, the Red Code stands. You will stand down, Shaya Costallion, right now.'

Shaya's eyes flashed and her lip curled. Her entire frame seemed to vibrate with fury and, for an instant, the Doctor thought she might shoot the mutineer where he stood.

But no; Shaya was a career soldier, of course. She had lived and breathed the rules and regulations since she was fourteen years old, and she knew that, however objectional and disloyal Cassio might be, he had acted according to protocol. His challenge had been legal and defensible, and the Doctor supposed that unless she wanted to find herself on trial for his murder, she had no choice but to acquiesce and bide her time. Her shoulders drooped in defeat, and she stepped back, letting her gun fall to her side.

The Doctor raised his hands in a pacifying gesture. 'I think perhaps we should all just calm down.'

Cassio flashed him a venomous glare. 'And you will be silent, or you will be shot.'

The new commander turned to his troops, and tapped his holo display so that Aliss could also follow his words.

'Clearly,' he said, 'there is something at work. Clearly, bodies have been broken by some kinetic force, manipulated either by Fenly or by something in collusion with, or in control of her.'

He strode across the room, passing Aliss, who turned to watch him as he headed for the opposite wall.

'No,' Belinda said. 'Don't!'

Cassio ignored her. He reached the far wall and turned to face the rest of them. 'And I maintain, if it exists, we will bring this entity into the open. We will examine it and, if necessary, we will execute it. Trooper 2?'

Kai snapped to attention. 'Yes, sir?'

'Do you volunteer to engage?'

'Yes, sir!'

The Doctor shook his head. 'I'm telling you, don't—'

Cassio pointed his gun at him. 'One more word,' he warned.

The Doctor closed his mouth. He could argue with a person, but he couldn't argue with a laser pulse.

'Either we disprove this story,' Cassio said, addressing the room, 'or we meet the enemy. Prepare to engage.'

Gun still raised at Aliss, he began to step sideways, to bring himself into a line with Aliss and Kai.

Everyone held their breath. Aliss was looking at Cassio, which meant she had her back to all of them. They were all in danger. And still Cassio moved.

'Don't look,' the Doctor muttered to Belinda and Mo.

'Shut up!' Cassio told him.

Cassio took another sideways pace, and Aliss shuffled around to keep looking at him.

From Kai's point of view, Cassio had disappeared. Which meant that Kai was now standing directly behind Aliss, looking at the back of her head.

He stared at Aliss, trying to see if there was anything there. Was that a shadow between her shoulder blades or a trick of the light?

He swallowed nervously, knowing this was the point when—

Suddenly, Kai *saw* it.

And it was more horrible than he could ever have imagined.

He opened his mouth to scream, and something flashed between him and Aliss. The air between them seemed to shudder, as if forces were at work beneath the skin of reality.

Twisting. Aching. Demanding…

'Look at it, Trooper,' Cassio demanded. 'What's behind her? What can you see?'

Kai couldn't speak. It felt as if time had slowed and yet he'd started to tremble.

Then he flailed about as if shaken in the grip of some vast clawed hand that tightened about him.

As a scream finally tore loose from his lips, Kai was launched across the room.

Sweating, hearts broken, the Doctor had known what was coming. He, Mo, Shaya and Trooper 5 had been keeping their eyes on the deck, but at the sound of the scream, everyone in the room looked up. Of course they did; how could they help it?

'Stop!' The Doctor warned them.

Kai flew in an arc over Aliss's head, straight towards Cassio.

'Don't move!' Belinda yelled.

Eyes wide, Cassio dived to the side just in time.

'No,' the Doctor shouted. 'Stop!'

Kai hit the wall with a bone-crunching smack and fell to the deck, dead.

'*Stop!*'

Aliss turned to keep her eyes on Cassio, which meant her back turned towards the rest of them. The Doctor and Belinda instinctively kept their eyes down. But they weren't quite in a direct line with Aliss and Cassio.

Trooper 6 was.

The man who looked like a schoolteacher shrieked in horror and hurtled upwards, arms and legs windmilling – and, just like Kai, flew straight for Cassio.

Cassio scrambled out of the way again, but that now brought the very tall Trooper 5 into alignment.

Even as 6 crashed violently into the deck, breaking his neck on impact, 5 gasped and was also wrenched into the air. Screaming, she arced towards Trooper 9, who was forced to leap aside, almost colliding with the grey-haired Trooper 8.

The older man staggered back, eyes wild. 'No way,' he said. 'No way.'

Giving in to panic, he turned and ran for the hatch. Unfortunately, Cassio had moved again, trying to stop the chain reaction he'd set off – and that now brought the hatch into a perfect line behind Aliss.

If Trooper 8 had kept going, he might have made it. But as he reached the threshold, he turned and glanced back.

And he saw the *thing*.

With a despairing cry, he flipped up and back, somersaulting the entire width of the room, causing Cassio to roll aside.

Trooper 8 slammed into the deck with sickening force. Even from thirty feet away, the Doctor heard every bone in the man's body shatter like crystal.

Dazed, Cassio staggered to his feet.

This would have brought Trooper 7 into alignment, but 7 was smart. He sidestepped, keeping his commander in sight, not hidden by Aliss.

That was when Shaya saw her chance. She had to put a stop to this before anyone else died.

'Aliss,' she said, but Aliss couldn't hear her. Squaring her shoulders, she strode across the room, radiating calm and control. As she moved, she tapped her holo display twice and said, 'Cast to Trooper 1.'

She reached the spot where Trooper 7 stood, shaken, and tapped the holo again.

'Aliss, turn one hundred and eighty degrees,' she said.

The words appeared on Cassio's chest. He stopped staggering, steadied himself and looked down, puzzled, trying to read them upside down. But Aliss had already read them and, before he could react, she turned around quickly to look at Shaya.

Now, from Shaya's point of view, Cassio was standing slightly to Aliss's left. His mouth fell open as he realised what was about to happen.

He locked eyes with Shaya.

'No,' he said.

She remained coldly expressionless, giving him an instant to understand what was about to happen. Then she stepped smartly to her right, hiding him behind Aliss.

There was a crash and a scream, and he went flying – up and over, tumbling through the air until he hit the back wall like a bug hitting a windscreen.

Bones pulverised, he fell dead to the deck.

For a long moment, nobody dared move or speak. Now there was nobody behind Aliss. She was facing them all.

Did that mean it was over?

Belinda hardly dared breathe.

Then Shaya broke the silence. 'I had to.'

Nobody replied. They were still in shock from the rapid cascade of violence and death.

'I had to,' she continued. 'He was out of control.'

The Doctor sighed. 'That's what it turns us into,' he said sadly, remembering how it had poisoned the minds of the tourists in the rover, all that time ago, turning them against each other and coaxing out their most selfish, murderous impulses. 'Put your gun down, Shaya. Please. Step back.'

Miraculously, Shaya lowered her weapon. He could see by the way she clenched her jaw that she was fighting back the devastation she felt at having killed her second-in-command, but the defiance in her eyes told him she still thought she'd done the right thing. The hard but necessary thing. And, much as he wanted to be angry with her, he recognised a little of himself in that expression.

And he hated it.

Silently, the survivors gathered at the hatch, all keeping their eyes on Aliss, trying not to let their eyes stray to the smashed and broken remains of their comrades and friends.

Still alone at the centre of the room, Aliss raised her hand and signed as she spoke, 'It's not my fault.'

The Doctor faced her, so she could see his words scrolling across his chest. 'I know. I really know.'

'But what do we do?' Belinda asked.

Shaya stepped forwards. With Cassio gone, the Doctor could see she was very much back in charge of the remaining members of her squad. And having seen how she'd dealt with him, he didn't think anyone else was going to try to pull a Red Code on her. Not now, not ever.

She tapped her holo on, so that Aliss could understand what she was saying as well, and addressed the room.

'We leave this place,' she said matter-of-factly. 'The mission has failed. We retreat.'

Aliss signed, *What about me?*

Shaya's expression didn't change. She might not have understood the sign, but she could read the woman's face. 'I'm sorry, you're contaminated.'

'But what about my daughter?'

Shaya turned away and deactivated her holo.

'We can't leave her behind,' Belinda protested, looking horrified at the idea.

'Can't we move her?' Mo asked, apparently also moved by Aliss's pleas. 'Okay, we can't step behind her, but can't we find some way to manoeuvre her somehow, and get her back to the ship?'

The Doctor glanced across the room. Unable to see their holos, Aliss squinted in concentration, and he guessed she was desperately trying to follow what they said by reading their lips.

He had not spoken up until this point. Now, he looked at those around him, and his expression was enough to silence them all.

'She is not leaving this planet with that thing,' he said in a voice that brooked no argument. 'Because that's what it wants. To escape. To leave here. To get out.'

'But we can't abandon her,' Belinda protested.

A ghost of a smile played across the Doctor's lips. 'That's not what I said.'

'Please,' Aliss said. 'Please don't turn away from me. Don't turn your backs on me.'

The Doctor turned and signed, *I'm sorry*.

It was time he took charge of this situation.

He inhaled a deep, cleansing breath and all the light in the room seemed to gather around him, drawing every eye.

He took a step forwards, and then another.

Shaya ordered, 'Doctor, stay where you are.'

'Too many people have died,' he told her, waving her objections away with a flick of his hand. 'And now, it *stops*.'

He tapped on his holo display and took another slow, careful step.

'I am addressing the thing behind Alice Fenly,' he said.

Another step.

'My old friend,' he continued. 'Do you remember me? Because I've never forgotten you. And now, you've waited 400,000 years. But who are you?'

He reached out and took Aliss's hand.

She stared up at him with helpless eyes. He could tell that she trusted him, but barely dared to hope he might be able to save her.

The Doctor gave her a reassuring smile, and then let his gaze slide slowly, so very slowly, sideways, until he was focused on the edge of her left ear.

'Are you there?' he asked.

His hearts were really beating now. The last time he'd met this thing, it had paralysed him, stealing away his words, leaving him as immobile and helpless as a puppet, unable to fight or otherwise resist.

The air behind Aliss began to stir, and there was a sense of pressure building, as in the atmosphere before a thunderstorm.

The suggestion of something vast and timeless about to materialise.

The Doctor found himself thinking of Earth's subway stations, and the blast of air that blew the length of the platform just before a train appeared.

Slowly, he leant further to the left.

Something was there but barely visible, like a shadow seen from the corner of the eye.

He narrowed his eyes, trying to focus on it.

Was it a shadow, or the very outermost edge of something? Maybe just the suggestion of a presence.

'What are you?' he asked, edging around a little more, trying to get a better angle.

Did it have a shape? He couldn't make it out.

Did it have a head? And if it had a head, did it have a body?

Was the fabric on Aliss's shoulder being pulled back, as if a hand was slowly clawing its way up from behind her?

whisper

It was hardly loud enough to be called a sound, but the whole room heard it.

'What was that?' Belinda asked, her voice catching in fear.

Shaya was trying to keep her expression professional and neutral, but her cheeks had paled and the tension showed in her eyes. 'Did it say something?'

'Oh.' The Doctor's gaze shifted to Aliss. 'Maybe that's how you survived. Maybe you're alive because you can't hear it.'

She looked petrified. 'What's it saying?'

whisper whisper

The sound was no louder than that of a single leaf rustling in the wind. The Doctor leaned closer to Aliss's shoulder, trying to hear.

Closer still.

And a tear striped down his cheek.

whisper whisper whisper

He began to cry. And the cries turned into anguished sobs.

'What is it?' Belinda asked, alarmed. 'What's it saying?'

He straightened up and sniffed.

With a huge effort, he pulled himself together enough to turn and look at her. His face was wet. His eyes were red-rimmed, and when he spoke, it was in a tone she'd never heard from him before.

In a small, helpless voice, he said, 'It knows my name.'

Chapter 10
Liquid Mercury

An awful, familiar, unmistakable chill forced its way into the Doctor's head. The creature remembered him. All the secrets, all the lies. Every agonising, unbearable moment of the Time War, every sorrow and regret. And it whispered them to him now: every life he'd failed to save, every companion he'd lost, every sacrifice he'd been forced to make.

Even the name that must not, could not be uttered.

Oh, especially that.

Like any predator, it knew how to zero in and exploit a weakness.

With claws of burning ice, it reached into his soul and drew out every terror, every loss and defeat. It paraded them in an appalling, soul-shredding onslaught.

Any ordinary mortal would have had their sanity flensed off. But the Doctor was no ordinary mortal. He had lived his life in reverse. He had started his adventures old and frail and cantankerous, and now he was young and strong and idealistic. Even in the face of such an assault, his old stubbornness remained. He summoned every ounce of his strength, every beat of his two hearts, every ancient legacy of his race, every name or title conferred upon him. He had taken on the worst the universe could throw at him, and he had prevailed. This *thing* might be the scariest entity he had ever encountered, but he was the Doctor. He was the one who haunted the dreams of the wicked and the cruel, from one side of the universe to the other. He was a still point at the heart of creation; a singularity in the mathematics of the universe.

The last time he'd encountered this creature, he'd been filled with guilt and self-loathing, and it had been turned against him. But this time was different. This time, he was filled with love and light. All the love that two hearts could hold. And if the creature had a problem with that, well then, that was just too bad.

He forced himself to turn back and move closer still. His instincts were screaming at him, telling him that if he *did* see this creature, the sight would kill him instantly.

Yet he couldn't stop.

After all this time, he had to know.

He had to lay eyes upon it.

And so he edged his head even further to the left, craning to see around Aliss ...

And there it was.

Throughout his life, the Doctor had faced many enemies. Implacable, belligerent, remorseless beings that acted against everything he believed in.

This was something different.

Not hate, aggression, callousness or evil. This was far purer and infinitely more terrible.

This was horror.

The Doctor stared deep into the abyss and bared his teeth.

You can't eat me; I'll stick in your throat. You can't turn me against myself, because I have accepted who I am.

And then, through the shimmer and the curdled light, he saw the answer staring him in the face.

'Oh yes!'

'What?' cried Belinda.

'There it is,' he said, through the pain and the strain.

'What?' Shaya asked, needing to know but fearful of the answer.

He straightened up and, still facing the presence, took a step back.

He said, 'It's behind you.'

Reading his lips, Aliss signed, *I know.*

'No.' The Doctor held up a finger. 'I'm not talking to you. I'm addressing the thing behind you. And behind *that* …'

He stepped back and turned to the others with a smile.

'What is it?' Belinda asked. 'What did you see?'

The Doctor's grin widened. 'The way out!'

He glanced up and around the room, taking in the walls, the pipes and the panels. Even the broken furniture.

The whole layout of the place.

Oh, yeah!

Filled with sudden energy, he ran across the room, making sure not to pass behind Aliss, to where one of the thick sets of pipes emerged from the floor and disappeared into the ceiling. In a burst of manic energy, he grabbed a gasket and twisted it, opening a valve inside the pipe. Then, he half ran, half danced across to another pipe and yanked down a squeaky, rusty lever.

'And I'm the idiot,' he called over his shoulder, addressing the entire room, including the thing lurking out of sight. 'Because I forgot what kind of mine this is.' He dashed over to a third section of pipe and started unscrewing it. 'Everyone, get ready to run,' he called gleefully. 'And I mean, *run.*'

The pipe squealed as it turned, its thread almost rusted in place.

'Oh, we should never have taken off our helmets,' he muttered to himself. 'Belinda, we're going to have to move really, really fast. How many can we fit in the airlock at once?'

'Six,' Shaya said.

'There's seven of us.' He finished removing the section of pipe and let it clatter to the metal deck. 'Shaya, get ready with that pistol.'

Shaya reached down and pulled her sidearm from its holster. 'What for?'

All the pipes had begun to clank and gurgle now, reverberating through the ceiling and the floor.

'You're the best shot in the land,' the Doctor said. 'And I need you to fire. Twice.'

He darted back to stand beside her, facing Aliss, and activated his holo display.

'And now, I am talking to the thing behind Aliss Fenly.' Anger tightened his words. 'I have a question for you, you stone cold murderer. If the thing behind you is always destroyed, then what happens if the thing behind you … is *you*?'

He turned to Shaya and pointed to the back wall, behind Aliss. 'Left-hand junction.'

High up near the ceiling, a thick pipe clung horizontally to the bulkhead, linking two metal junction boxes, one on the pipe's left end and the other on the right.

Shaya fired a single shot and the first box blew noisily apart.

'Right-hand junction,' the Doctor said, and she fired again, punching a hole in the other.

For a second, nothing happened. Then the pressure flooding into the pipe from the rest of the system caused it to crack and begin to split apart from either end. The walls creaked and groaned, and suddenly bright silver liquid began to pour from either end of the gradually widening split, splashing onto the deck behind Aliss.

'Mercury,' the Doctor explained, pointing at Shaya. 'You said, this mine uses a line-drop made of mercury.'

Slowly, the two streams spread along the fractured pipe. Aliss began to swivel where she sat, trying to see what was happening, but he caught her attention with a wave and slapped a hand against his chest. 'Keep facing me.'

She bit her lip nervously, obviously aching to know what he had done, but trusting him enough that she didn't turn around.

The two leaks fell in gradually widening columns, moving towards each other as the split in the pipe grew wider like shimmering curtains closing at the end of a theatre performance.

With a gasp of sudden understanding, Mo said, 'It's going to reflect it!'

'Of course!' Belinda realised. 'It can't hide if it's in front of a mirror. That's why it broke them all.'

The Doctor grinned, pleased that they had caught on to his plan.

'What will it do to me?' Aliss asked plaintively.

The Doctor made sure his holo was on. 'Aliss, whatever it does,' he said, doing his best to convey reassurance and encouragement, 'you've got us. We are here for you, okay?'

The curtains were almost touching now, and the whole back wall was becoming a beautiful liquid mirror.

'Get ready,' he said to the others behind him. 'Eyes on Aliss.'

'Are we going to see it?' Shaya asked.

'Do we look?' Mo wanted to know.

'Do we look away?' Belinda asked.

The Doctor made a face. 'I don't know!'

The final section of pipe cracked open and the bright silver streams of liquid mercury collided and merged. The back wall became a single reflective surface, and, for the briefest instant, they caught a movement.

A ripple in the air.

The half-seen shadow creature gave a violent convulsion and threw Aliss forwards, hard and fast.

Belinda, Mo and the other troopers piled in from either side and managed to catch her before she hit the wall, and they all went down in a heap.

Aliss was free.

'Now, run!' the Doctor yelled. 'Run!'

Chapter 11
The Thing

They ran.

All seven of them, hurtling pell-mell back along Walkway Five and past the scattered bodies and empty bedrooms of Walkway Four. Their boots clattered and boomed on the echoing metal deck. The overhead lights flickered and guttered. Pipes squealed and protested. But on they ran, retracing their steps, jumping over corpses and stray pieces of equipment, neither pausing nor looking back until, as they came in sight of the airlock at the far end of Walkway One, the Doctor skidded to a halt.

He couldn't help it.

He had to take a look. He needed to see, and to know what was happening.

If he were ever to rest, the Doctor had to be certain that he'd finally vanquished the nightmare of Midnight.

Belinda slowed to a stop a little ahead of him and turned back. Together, they peered through the flickering light.

At first, there was nothing.

Then, there at the far end of Walkway Two, a sense of movement. A ripple in the air. A shadow where no shadow could be cast.

It was hard to see its shape or to focus on it, but there was definitely *something* there. Something moving on the floor. And it was … unfurling, like a flower.

The Doctor and Belinda exchanged a look: *Nuh-uh. No more of that.* Then they turned and raced after the others, running the length of Walkway One, back into the airlock's antechamber.

Shaya and Mo were already pushing the inner lock door shut. Troopers 7 and 9 were inside with Aliss, who now wore one of the base's helmets and bulky spacesuits. As the heavy door swung shut, she looked at the Doctor and signed, *Thank you.*

Then the hatch crunched shut, and the locks engaged with a heavy thump.

Shaya and Mo began helping the Doctor and Belinda into their armour and helmets.

'You should have got out,' the Doctor said.

'I am not leaving you behind,' Shaya told him. 'The flight-packs are dead, just run as far as you can!'

Mo was strapping the last piece of armour to Belinda's suit. 'Come on,' she muttered. 'Come on, come on.'

Behind them, the lights of Walkway One started to dim and sputter.

'Hurry up, hurry up,' Belinda urged, not sure if she was talking to Mo or herself. She didn't understand what she'd seen back there, but she knew with cold and certain clarity that it was after them.

That it was angry.

And it was coming.

The final clips clicked into place, and they were ready to go.

'Helmets,' Shaya instructed, holding one out to the Doctor. Even as he reached for it, a pressure wave roared down the corridor, shoving them all backwards and knocking them off their feet.

They hit the deck and the Doctor braced, expecting an attack.

But no attack came.

Nothing but silence.

They lay there, shaken, looking up at the unsteady overhead lights.

'What was that?' Mo asked as they climbed stiffly back to their feet.

Belinda winced as she dusted herself down. She would definitely have bruises tomorrow. 'Are we okay?'

Shaya narrowed her eyes as she regarded Mo with suspicion. 'What happened?'

'That wind.' Mo looked fearful. 'Was that the *thing*?'

'Doctor?' Belinda asked. 'Doctor, what happened?'

The Doctor didn't reply. He simply stood there, glaring into the darkness at the other end of Walkway One.

A ping came from behind them as the hatch disengaged.

'The others are out,' Mo said. 'The airlock's clear.'

Now the Doctor moved. Slowly, painfully, he shook his head. 'I'm sorry,' he said, and they could all feel the regret in his voice. 'But we're not going anywhere. We can't.'

Belinda's mouth fell open. They had been so close. 'No. You don't think …?'

The Doctor gave a regretful nod. 'It's here.'

Stomach twisting, Belinda looked wildly at Mo, then at Shaya. Could they be infected? Could the thing be standing behind them right now, as it had stood behind Aliss?

She saw her own fear reflected back in their stares, their eyes wide and suspicious.

'It's not me.' Mo's voice shook.

'Well, it's not me,' Shaya asserted.

'I swear,' Mo insisted. 'It's not me.' She shook her head. 'It really isn't me. It really, really isn't.'

The Doctor patted his chest, his stomach, his hip. He searched the corners of his peripheral vision. Nothing looked or felt amiss. No coldness, no whispers.

'I don't think it's me,' he said.

Like Shaya and Mo, he turned to Belinda.

She stood there by the airlock door, trembling. He could see she was trying to be brave, but also that she was terrified.

The Doctor sighed. 'Oh, Belinda.'

'No.' She screwed up her face. 'No, no, no.'

'But –' The Doctor took a step towards her, desperate for a way out of this situation. 'It might not be …'

Belinda's eyes opened wide, and her haunted look stopped him in his tracks. 'It's whispering,' she said, voice cracking. 'I can *hear* it.'

'Oh, Bel.' Sadness crashed over the Doctor. He'd known her such a brief time, but she was so strong, so *brilliant*, and he had promised, hadn't he? He'd made so many promises to get her home to her family.

'Is it behind me?' she asked.

He didn't want to look. He didn't want to see that creature again, and he especially didn't want to see it behind her, because that would mean he'd failed to protect her.

And the creature knew exactly how much that would hurt him.

But he had to know, he had no choice. Before he could decide anything else, he had to be certain it was there.

He moved his head to the left. And he saw it. The same shadow's edge. The same hint of a presence.

But now, there was something else as well.

Was that the merest suggestion, the flimsiest ghost, of … a *smile*?

The dismay and anger that clouded his face confirmed Belinda's worst fears. 'I'm sorry,' she said.

He shook his head so, so sadly. 'It's not your fault.'

It was all his mistake. He'd put her in harm's way and let the most loathsome, abhorrent entity in the universe sink its claws into her. And now, there was only one way he could set things right. Even though the thought made him sick with fear, he knew what he had to do.

He closed his eyes, inhaled a long breath through his nostrils. For a moment, he entertained all the dread and doubt, letting it saturate his nervous system and set his hearts racing. He experienced it all, drank it in, and then let it pass through him and away like a cloud scudding across the sky.

No second thoughts.

He thrust out his hand. 'Take me,' he said.

Belinda's eyes went wide. 'No!'

'Whatever you are,' he demanded, chin raised defiantly, 'stand behind me.'

'No,' she said. 'Doctor, don't.'

'I promised to keep you safe,' he told her. 'And now I am telling the thing behind you. You've seen into my mind. You know how I travel. How powerful I am. So I'm offering you a deal. A simple one. You can walk the universe on my back. If, *and only if*, you set her free.'

The pressure returned, and the air between them seemed to congeal.

whisper whisper

The Doctor shuddered. The breathy rasp lingered on the very edge of audibility, but nevertheless conveyed an unmistakable, terrible satisfaction.

Triumph.

After half a million years of solitude, the entity knew it was finally going to leave its barren prison and fly among the stars, spreading itself to all the strange new worlds it had glimpsed in the Doctor's memories, all that time ago.

It would feel and grow and spread to every lantern in the sky.

Nothing could stop it now.

Nothing in the universe.

Chapter 12
Through Flames and Chaos and Ruin

The Doctor braced himself, uncertain of how the entity would pass to him. Of course, he would never take the thing anywhere inhabited. One single journey was all he'd provide – pushing the TARDIS beyond her tolerances to the beginnings of the universe or to the end of creation. There would be a finish to this horror, and no one else would be harmed.

Except, the entity knew him. Knew everything he was. It must sense his intentions and have ideas of its own of how to thwart them …

'Doctor,' Shaya said in brisk, clipped tones. 'The physical construction of this human race. Is it similar to Lombardic?'

'What?'

She was all business now. A professional soldier, completely in control. 'Is the torso constructed the same?'

He squeezed his eyebrows together, wracking his memory. 'Yes, basically.'

She unholstered her pistol. 'Then a shot fired three millimetres above the superior vena cava of the heart could mean death, or it could mean the narrowest chance of survival.'

She brought the gun up to point at Belinda's chest.

'No.' The Doctor realised what she was planning, and the risk horrified him. 'No, no, don't!'

'Don't do it!' Mo shouted.

'You can't,' Belinda protested, backing away, staring down the barrel of Shaya's gun. 'No, you can't!'

'All you need,' Shaya said, 'is a very good shot.'

She stepped between the Doctor and Belinda, her gun aimed directly at Belinda's heart.

Behind her, the Doctor squirmed, not wanting this to happen, acutely aware that the margin of error was so small – the difference between life and death less than a hair's breadth – but nevertheless needing Shaya to try.

Not for his own sake, nor even entirely for Belinda's.

For the sake of all the souls that would suffer if this thing ever truly escaped Midnight.

Beyond Shaya, Belinda stood upright and still.

As a nurse, the Doctor knew she must understand what Shaya was hoping to do. He could see she was frightened, but she was in control.

'It'll go to you,' she warned the other woman.

Shaya's posture remained unwavering. 'I'm a soldier,' she said. 'This is my job.'

The Doctor watched, breath held as, for an unbearable moment, they remained frozen in this ghastly tableau, both agreeing on what needed to be done, but frightened of the consequences.

Belinda raised her chin. 'Do it.'

Mo gasped and covered her mouth with her hand.

Shaya closed one eye, sighted and fired. A white hot needle of laser fire speared Belinda through the chest. She tottered back on her heels for an instant, and then slumped back like a marionette with its strings cut.

The lights flickered.

Something moved through the air, too fast for the eye to focus. Shaya lowered her gun and gasped.

The Doctor pushed past her. He stared at Belinda in shock. She lay sprawled on the ground, a thin line of grey smoke rising from the burned edges of the hole through the front of her suit. His nostrils flinched at the acrid smells of charred fabric and singed flesh.

No, no, no ...

She lay still, eyes closed, unbreathing. The laser bolt had taken her right through the heart.

Surely, an instant kill-shot.

He put a hand to his mouth.

No ....

He had lost her.

A tear ran down his cheek.

Oh Bel, I'm so, so sorry ...

Then she jerked. Her feet kicked and her eyes flew open. She gasped raggedly for air.

Mo was the first to recover from the shock. She ran for one of the emergency medical kits on the wall by the lock.

The Doctor knelt and took Belinda's hand. 'I've got you,' he whispered, a tear falling onto her cheek. 'I've got you.'

'Med lines!' Mo shouted. 'Her heart isn't beating. Get outta the way!'

She pulled white defibrillator cables from the kit on the wall and dragged them towards Belinda. They were designed to use a high-energy jolt to restart the hearts of crewmembers who were in cardiac arrest, whether caused by a heart attack, injury or suit malfunction on the surface.

The Doctor got up and backed away to let Mo work. The trooper opened a patch in Belinda's suit, just below her collar bone, so she could apply the paddles.

Then he saw Shaya turn and run back into the depths of the base.

The Doctor gave a shout of frustration. He couldn't bear to leave Belinda, but whatever Shaya was doing …

He turned to Mo. 'Power up to sixty and apply the cables to the heart five times.' Then he turned and hurtled after the fleeing Platoon Leader.

Shaya ran.

Her legs were tired, her heart thumped and her pulse raced, but she was in good shape. She had always trained hard and now, despite her fatigue, if she had to, she could run a marathon.

Not that she planned to run that far.

Her objective was the Central Control Room. Her mission was to protect the last survivors of her squad and perhaps the whole galaxy, from the awful thing behind her.

Her boots hammered against the deck plates.

Not much further now.

She knew Chinchappa had given her this mission because he'd had doubts about her fitness for command. She was a model soldier but, sometimes, she hesitated. She took too long to think through important decisions.

So he'd given her this easy search-and-rescue mission to see how she coped, and appointed Cassio as her second-in-command to keep an eye on her, and initiate a Red Code if he felt it necessary.

The trouble was, Cassio had always been reckless and ambitious. Shaya should have expected that he'd try to oust her the first excuse he got. His arrogance and inability to anticipate consequences had caused the deaths of half her squad. She'd taken no pleasure in killing him but felt no regret either; he'd got what he deserved.

Now it was her turn to die. But Shaya knew she'd be going out on her own terms, in the performance of her duty: saving colleagues and civilians, protecting her home world and defeating an enemy.

That would show Chinchappa.

It would show all of them.

She had been fighting since she was a kid. She knew how capable she was. And she knew in her heart that Cassio would never have had the courage to do what she was about to do.

And so she ran.

With a rush of adrenalin, she felt fourteen years old again: the fastest sprinter on her planet, running through burning Wildlands, the wind straggling out her hair and the smoke irritating her eyes and throat. Running like a wild spirit through flames and chaos and ruin …

My name is serving officer Shaya Costallion, Squadron 775, she told herself. *I ran as a child. I ran from the Wildlands. I ran from those monsters and never looked back. And I ran across the galaxy with one aim: to do my duty, to help, to protect, to bring hope.*

The Doctor burst into the Central Control Room and skidded to a stop. Shaya stood with her back to the gaping, seemingly bottomless Well in the centre of the room, the heels of her boots almost overhanging the edge of the void.

Both breathing hard from exertion, they regarded each other the way old soldiers sometimes do. A respectful understanding passed between them.

He wanted to tell her to step away from the edge, but he knew she wouldn't. Once again, as she had when she'd killed Cassio, she had made the hard but necessary choice. She knew what the mission required, and she had determined to do it.

He gave her a nod, to let her know it was okay and that she wasn't alone.

That he cared.

With the ghost of a smile, still holding his gaze, she let herself tip backwards until she fell soundlessly into the hole and vanished from sight.

The Doctor threw himself at the edge of the Well, skidding across the floor on his chest until his head and shoulders stuck out above the shaft.

'No!' he yelled into the darkness.

It was so unfair!

Why couldn't there have been another way, a different choice?

'No!' His voice echoed down the borehole, into the timeless, stygian depths of the planet.

Back at the airlock, Belinda stared up at the ceiling, her body numb, mind reeling. She'd been shot through the heart! The creature must have assumed she was a goner and fled to Shaya. She knew that her chances of survival were very small. But she'd be damned if she'd go gently into the night. She was going to fight for every breath and every fleeting millisecond of life. No way would she end up as just another corpse in this terrible mausoleum, a footnote to the massacre of the mine workers. She had things to live for. Her parents were waiting, back in London. She couldn't die here like this, not now. She couldn't let them spend the rest of their lives wondering what had happened to her and why she'd disappeared.

She was vaguely aware that Mo was pressing something to her chest. Shadows seemed to be gathering at the corners of her eyes. She couldn't remember how long it had been since she'd last taken a breath.

A kind of weird calm settled over her like a shroud.

She felt the deck shake beneath her. Footsteps running this way.

And then the Doctor was there, out of breath and leaning over her, his deep eyes wide with worry and his face streaked with tears.

And somehow, she knew then. It was over.

The Doctor was alive.

And Belinda dared to believe she might pull through as well.

Blinking in and out of consciousness, Belinda saw the rescue ship batter its way down through the radioactive atmosphere. Distantly she felt the thrum through the ground as it touched down.

She heard the Doctor persuading the surviving troopers to help him carry her to the doors of the TARDIS. Then he'd helped her inside to its sanctuary by himself.

When she woke properly, Belinda was lying on the floor beside the main console. Two white cables, similar to the ones Mo had used in the base – but, according to the Doctor, infinitely more sophisticated – stretched from an open panel in the console's supporting column to a large field dressing on her chest.

The Doctor was at her side, keeping her calm. 'It's okay, it's okay,' he kept repeating. 'I've got you. I've got you, Bel.' She wasn't sure if he was trying to reassure her, or himself.

'My heart ...' she croaked.

'Is fine,' he told her. 'We got you in time. Now it's pumped full of super-skin-stitch.' He squeezed her arm. 'All mending.'

She felt a flood of relief. 'Okay.' The muscles in her arms and legs relaxed, and her fists unclenched. Somehow, he had got her out of that base, and it looked like she was going to be all right. She was going to live; she was going to see her mum and dad again.

But . . .

'What happened back there?' she asked. 'With the thing?'

'It's gone,' the Doctor said.

She was almost afraid to ask. 'And Shaya?'

'I'm sorry.' He looked away. 'I couldn't save her. I tried. But she threw herself into the mineshaft, taking that creature with her, to save us all.'

Belinda's vision fuzzed with tears. 'Did it work?' she asked. 'Are we safe?'

The Doctor smiled. 'Yes,' he said.

She lay there for a while with the Doctor beside her, in an easy silence.

During her time as a nurse, Belinda had only seen a couple of gunshot victims, but she understood enough about them to know that, unlike in the movies, you couldn't simply bounce back from penetrating wounds like that. And yet, she could already feel the itch of the super-skin-stitch as it busied itself

146

in her heart, knitting together her seared flesh and closing the wounds. Perhaps, she thought, she was going to be well again much more quickly than she expected.

A miracle cure from a miraculous man. No wonder they called him the Doctor.

She smiled, but even as she started to relax, a new fear gripped her and she reached out to him.

'But Shaya and Mo,' she said. 'They'd never heard of the Earth. They'd never heard of human beings.' She swallowed, afraid to ask. 'Doctor, what's happened to the Earth?'

She watched his face, could see him considering how best to respond. How to spare her feelings, perhaps.

'I don't know,' he admitted finally.

The Doctor was already thinking through his next moves. When Belinda was recovered, he'd take the Vindicator reading they had gathered on the surface of Midnight and feed that data into the TARDIS systems to see whether it made a difference. In theory, the more readings he supplied the old girl, the easier it would be for her to pinpoint the correct temporal and spatial landing coordinates.

But if the Earth *had* somehow disappeared in the meantime, how could she get a lock on something that wasn't there any more?

Shaya and Mo should have heard of the human race. At this point in history, Earth and Lombardo ought to have been staunch allies. The fact that none of the Lombardic soldiers had recognised the name at all suggested something very, very worrying had happened and that, somehow, the Earth had vanished from the picture long before the Lombardics had a chance to encounter it.

Belinda was staring up at the lights rippling on the control room's dome-like ceiling. 'How does the Earth not exist …?' she murmured.

The Doctor had no answer, and that worried him more than he wanted her to see. Some sort of catastrophic event had distorted the timeline, and he didn't know how or why. All he could do was lie on the floor next to her and hold her hand.

Together they stared upwards like frightened children, feeling small and lost and scared.

Epilogue
Debriefing

Out here between the stars, no sunrise or sunset marked the passage of time. According to the troop carrier's clocks, it was late evening, and so the computer had artificially dimmed the internal lights to simulate the coming of night.

Most of the damage the vessel had suffered during its descent into Planet 6-7-6-7's atmosphere had been fixed, or at least patched up. The engines still ran raggedly after their exposure to the galvanic radiation, but they would probably last long enough to get the ship and its surviving personnel back to Lombardo.

Most of those personnel, including the remaining soldiers from Shaya's platoon, were now in their bunks, catching up on some well-earned rest.

All except Trooper 3, Mo Gilliben.

She had been summoned to the Comms Room for debriefing. As the highest-ranking survivor of the mission, it was her responsibility to provide the official account of events.

So, instead of falling into her bed like the others and closing her eyes, she found herself perched in an uncomfortable chair, relaying her account of the mission to a senior officer on another ship, light years away.

'… And Platoon Leader Shaya Costallion should be recommended for posthumous recognition,' she said, fighting to keep a tremor of emotion from her voice. 'Bravery in the face of impossible odds.'

She paused, remembering her last sight of her platoon leader, as Shaya charged from the room, sidearm still smoking in her hand, to save them all. It had been the bravest, most noble and tragic act she'd ever witnessed.

'And Cassio,' she added. 'I mean, Trooper Palin-Paleen. He tried his best.' There was no point in smearing his record; they had all been way out of their depths, and she couldn't blame him for screwing up. 'Once we were safe, the Doctor gave orders for us to follow Cassio's original advice and nuke the entire site from orbit. He said it was the only way to be sure. Nuke the site and never return.'

The orbital bombardment had been spectacular. As a small transport ship, the troop carrier could only field a brace of tactical battlefield nukes, and Mo had insisted the crew used both to target the mining installation. Even from a thousand miles up, the flashes were bright enough to sear glowing purple after-images into her retinas.

At the centre of those twin detonations, Colony Base 15 and the corpses it contained had been completely vaporised and the rock beneath heated into molten lava. The lava had then flowed across the entire site, sealing the mineshaft and hopefully burying that *creature* for ever.

On the screen, Officer Flood was considering Mo's testimony.

Flood was a mature woman with smartly tied-back grey hair and piercing eyes that stared out from a narrow, lined face. She wore an immaculate red and black dress uniform with no insignia or indication of rank. Mo hadn't encountered her before, and wasn't entirely sure who she was or how she slotted into the chain of command. But Flood was an officer and Mo was just a lowly Trooper. It wasn't her place to ask questions, and that was all there was to it.

'And this Doctor,' Flood said, voice clipped, brisk and efficient. 'What do we know about him?'

Mo felt confused. 'We thought he was sent by you.'

Surely, he'd waved around some kind of official identification that showed he had been working for Military Intelligence? At the time, she'd been certain that's what his ID card had said.

But funnily enough, when she tried to picture it now, she couldn't.

'He'd got this sort of ... cargo, on the ship,' she said. 'A big, tall blue box.'

Flood raised an eyebrow.

'Was he carrying this?' she asked, and a picture of the device Belinda had referred to as a 'Vindicator' appeared on the screen. An aerial with straps.

'Um, yes,' Mo confirmed, confused but intrigued. 'Yes, he was.'

'Well, that's exactly what I needed to know.' Flood spoke kindly, but there was a steely edge to her tone. 'Just as I predicted. A Vindicator, in action.' Her eyes burned with satisfaction. 'That's very good news for the future of the species.' She smiled. 'Thank you, Mo.'

Dismissed, Mo rose to leave. At that moment, she felt a sort of subsonic clang deep in her diaphragm, and her ears became aware of a creaking, groaning *vworp, vworp* noise.

It was coming from below, from the box where she'd left Belinda.

'Excuse me,' she said to the woman on the screen, and turned to run.

Down the stairs and gangways she raced, skidding around corners and flinging herself down companionways, until she got to the jump deployment corridor. Crashing through the hatch, she stumbled to a halt just in time to see the strange wooden box grow transparent and vanish into the air, leaving only a wheezing echo to show it had ever been there at all.

And then, when the reverberation of its engines had whispered away into complete silence, the only trace to remain was a gentle stir as the air in the corridor settled to fill the space vacated by the box.

'What the hell?'

Mo stepped forwards and reached out, thinking the object, whatever it was, might have activated some sort of cloaking device or invisibility shield, but her hand encountered only emptiness.

Exhausted and bewildered, she stared at the now-vacant alcove where the box had been nestling flush with the wall. She had really liked Belinda and had hoped they might become better friends. But now that her new friend had literally disappeared into thin air without so much as a goodbye ...

Talk about being ghosted!

As she stood there, dumbfounded, the hatch at the other end of the corridor clunked open and Trooper 11 – Val – poked her head in.

'What was that noise?'

Mo gave a tired sigh. 'Do you know what, Val? I've got absolutely no idea.' She shrugged. 'I don't think I know anything any more.'

Val gave her a concerned look. 'Are you okay, Mo? It sounds like you went through a nightmare down there.'

'Nightmare?' Mo gave a mirthless chuckle. 'That's the word, yeah. *Nightmare.*' She shook her head; so much had taken place, but so little of it had made any kind of sense. 'I've got to write the report, and I couldn't tell you what happened. I wouldn't even know where to start.' She smiled in a *what-can-you-do* kind of way.

Val didn't smile back. She didn't even seem to have heard her properly. She just stood there, staring.

Mo felt the hairs rise on the nape of her neck. 'What?'

Val frowned, brows drawing together and eyes narrowing. 'Nothing …'

'No, really.' Mo's chest went tight and she couldn't seem to get enough air. 'What is it?'

But Val didn't answer. She just stared, trying to focus on something just past Mo's left shoulder.

Something behind her.

Acknowledgements

I first started watching *Doctor Who* in the 1970s, when Tom Baker was the Doctor. In those days, there were no repeats or streaming services, or even videos to purchase. When an episode aired on a Saturday night, you knew you had to cram every moment of the action into your brain – because once the credits rolled at the end it was gone, and there was no way to watch it again.

In fact, the only way to re-experience those adventures, and others I'd never seem from the Doctor's earlier incarnations, was via the Target novelisations in the local library. In a sense, those Target novels were as much *Doctor Who* as the TV show itself, and my first introduction to many of the classic companions and monsters. I read those books over and over again until I had practically memorised them, word for word.

So, how does it feel to actually *write* a Target novelisation, all these years later?

It's the achievement of a 45-year-old dream. I only wish I had a TARDIS so I could go back to 1979 and tell my ten-year-old self all about it. He would absolutely freak out!

I would like, therefore, to say a huge thank you to my agent, Lucienne Diver at the Knight Agency, for getting me this opportunity. To my editor, Steve Cole, and to Shammah Banerjee and the team at Penguin Random House. To Russell T Davies and Sharma Walfal, who wrote the original script. To my wife Dianne for all her love and support, and to my daughters Edith and Rose for their belief and enthusiasm.

And lastly, to everyone who has done their part on either side of the screen to keep *Doctor Who* alive and in our hearts.

Also available in the Target series from BBC Books

DOCTOR WHO

LUX

JAMES GOSS

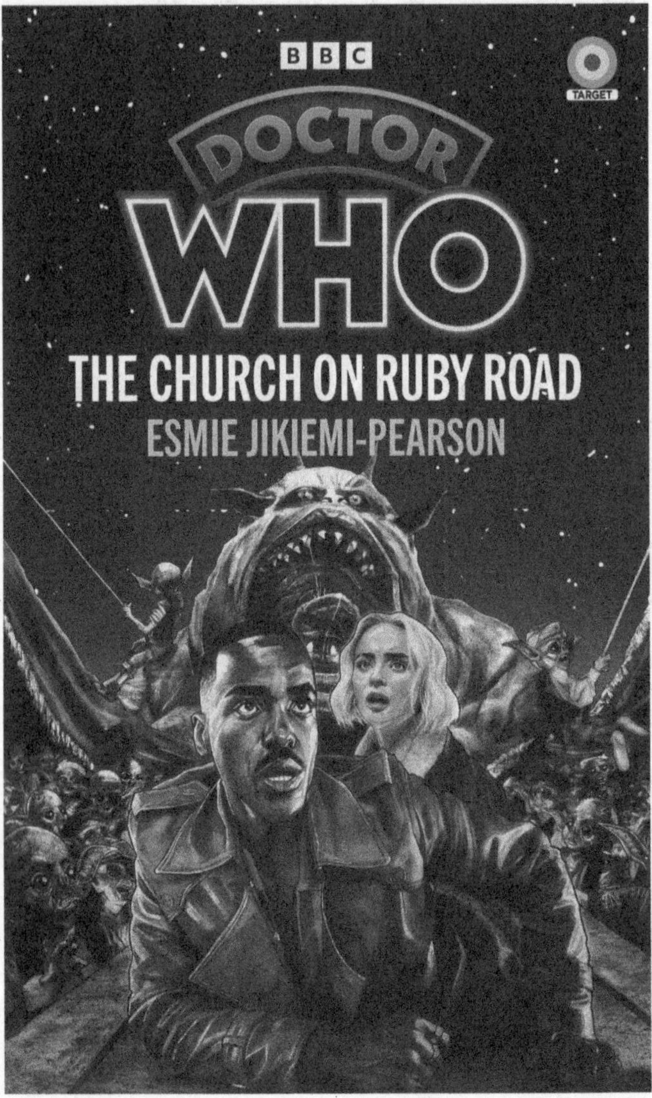
BBC
TARGET
DOCTOR
WHO
THE CHURCH ON RUBY ROAD
ESMIE JIKIEMI-PEARSON

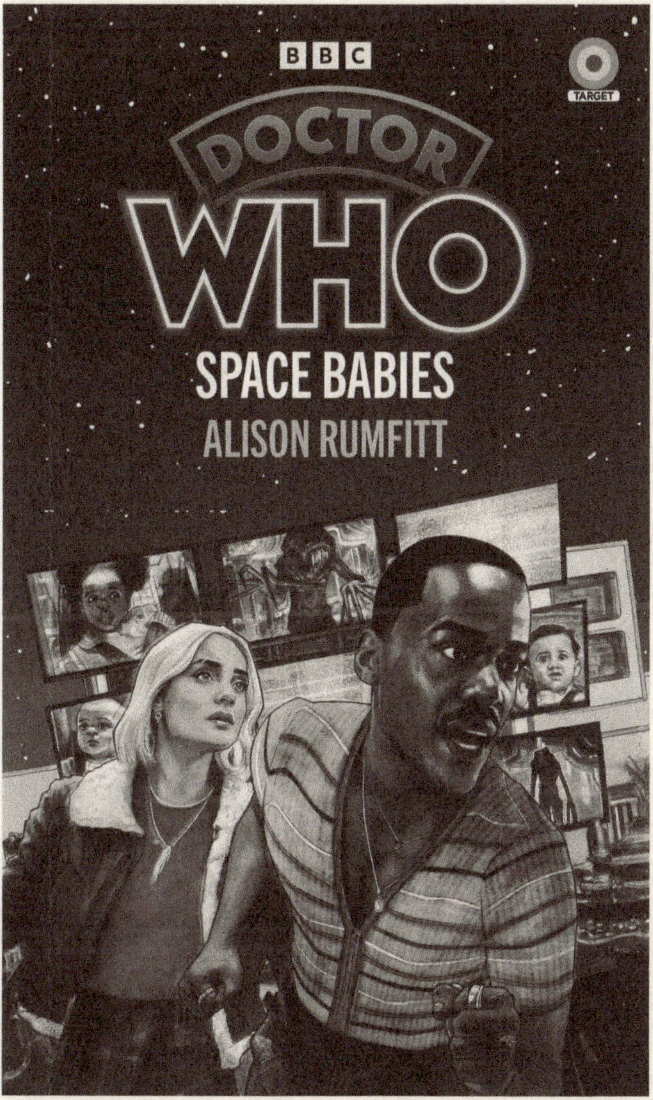
BBC
TARGET
DOCTOR
WHO
SPACE BABIES
ALISON RUMFITT

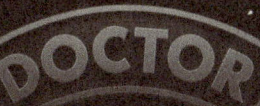

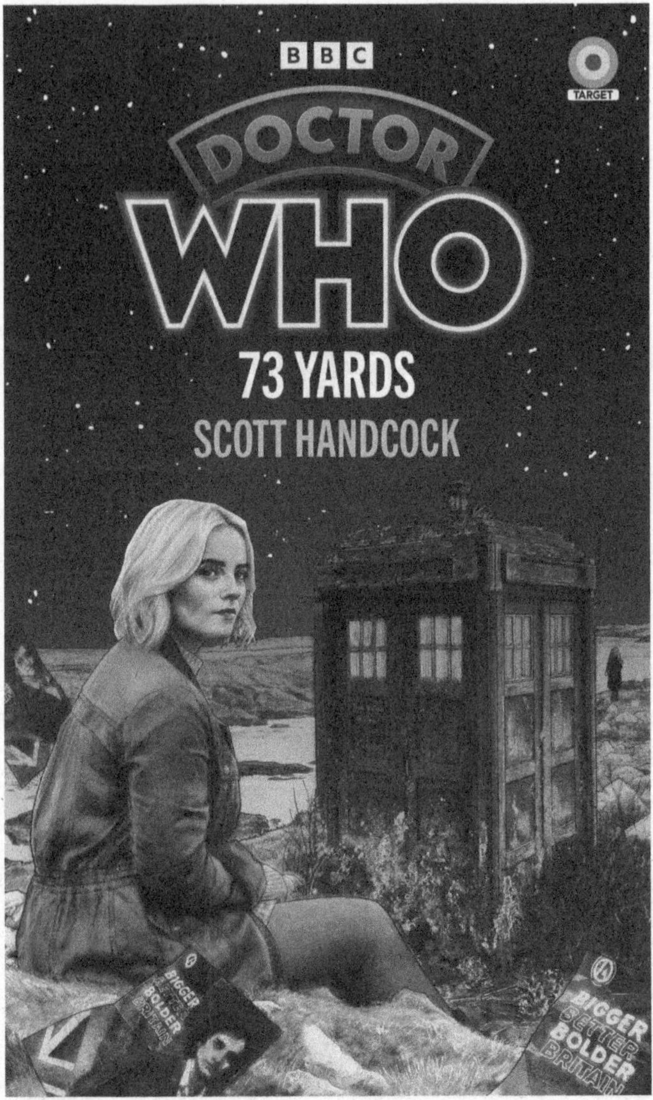
BBC
TARGET
DOCTOR
WHO
73 YARDS
SCOTT HANDCOCK
BIGGER
BETTER
BOLDER
BRITAIN

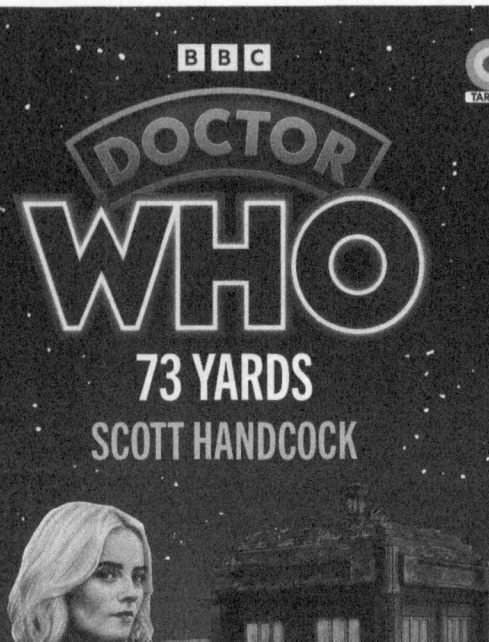

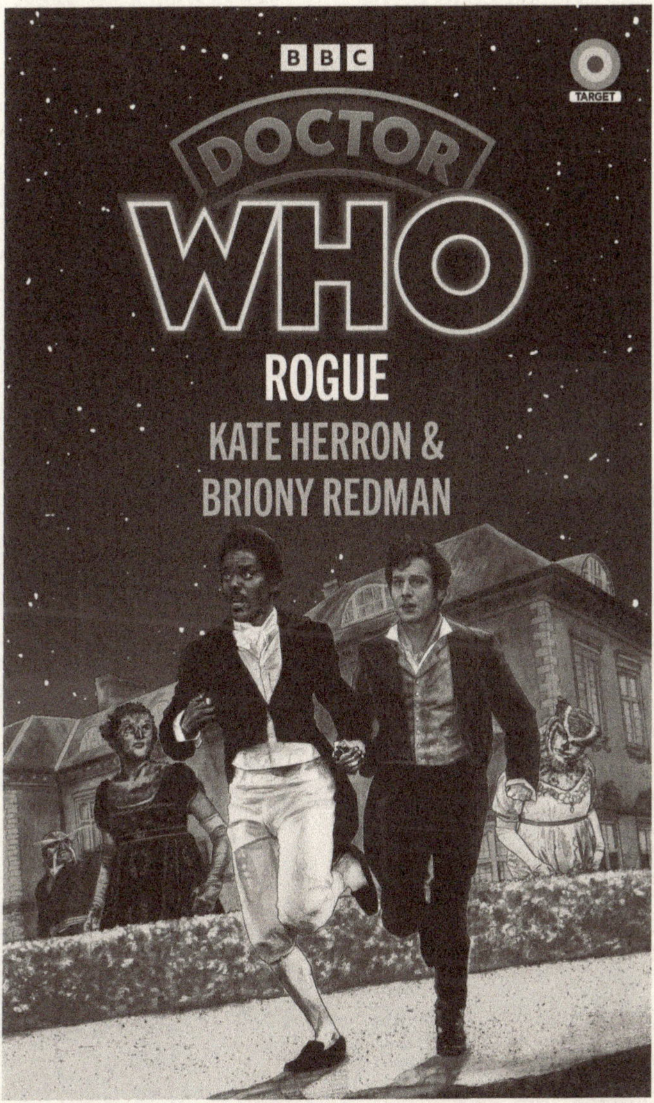
BBC
TARGET
DOCTOR WHO
ROGUE
KATE HERRON &
BRIONY REDMAN

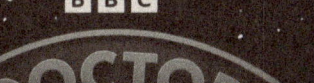

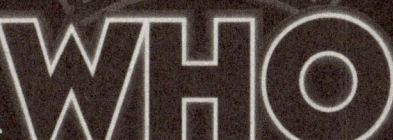